THE TEXAN: HARROWING

THE TEXAN: HARROWING

DANIEL E. OLIVAREZ

atmosphere press

Dedicated to the Memory of
Christopher Russell

You've touched so many lives, including mine. Thank you for the memories, dude! See you on the other side...

FOREWORD

When I was first asked to read this book and give my thoughts on it, I took great honor in being asked to do something so personal. I have known the author for about twenty years, so not only was I helping out a fellow writer with his burgeoning project, but I was helping out a friend as well. That being stated, I had absolutely no context as to what the book was even about or what to expect.

I received the email with a draft of the book during a busy time in my life, and I let the author know it would take me a while to get to it but that I'd be honest with my opinions for the good of his project. Once I was able to calmly go through the pages of the draft, I was introduced to the main character. He was someone who felt like a familiar presence in my life growing up but also had layers completely foreign to me, and I trusted him to take me on whatever journey on which he was about to embark. I was not ready for the twists and turns the story took, something reminiscent of action movies from the 80s and 90s that I would watch with my father and brother or my buddies, and the whole book played out in my head like a fun popcorn film I would be willing to watch over and over again.

I cannot wait to see what kind of story "The Texan" will get himself into with his wits, skills, determination, and that indomitable Texan spirit, and I am hoping to see the growth that the author, character, and audience will experience in future installments.

ORLANDO CAMPA, Screenwriter

Chapter 1
Houston, TX, 2014

Busy day as usual at George Bush Intercontinental Airport.

Thousands of people going to and from their destinations from one side of the terminal to the next.

Although most of the passengers were of Spanish descent, there were others whom Airport security would find questionable during these times of the epidemic.

Muslim visitors coming home to see their sons or daughters who worked in the city. African-Americans who had just returned from a seminary trip to Africa.

Security measures were raised high during the Ebola panic, nowadays nobody in a uniform was taking any risks when it came to a man returning from Africa wearing a face mask.

Same routine as always, the typical "Sir, could you step over here please?" while other uniforms closed in on him. After that, the man was not seen again.

Walking past the uniformed guards, not paying attention to the curious onlookers who always wanted to stick their noses in other people's business, a mysterious, quiet man carrying only a small military duffel bag over his right shoulder and a bag of sour patch kids in his left hand made his way towards a United Airlines flight heading to Cairns International Airport in Queensland, Australia, with a stop in Los Angeles to connect flights.

He was a moderate build; 5'10" who seemed by his appearance to work out on a daily basis. He also had two tattoos, one on each of his arms, but no more than that. He was also bald with a chinstrap beard, but no mustache. By the look of his appearance to others he might be a marine who was returning from duty overseas. The only exception was he wasn't returning from anywhere.

'DELAYED,' said the screen that showed all departing flights.

"Shit!" mumbled the quiet man.

It was bad enough he had to wake up at 6:00am for a flight that was supposed to leave at 9:50am. Now the new departure time was 10:50am, all he could do now was wait at a bar near the gate and drink his time away.

It was a sports bar paying tribute to Houston's very own Texans, with various customers dressed to honor their favorite football team.

The man didn't care much for football, give him baseball or hockey and he was game. He remembered growing up and playing in cul-de-sacs and alleyways in New York or various cities that he had visited growing up. Unfortunately for him, it was hard to make friends. Since he moved around a lot, he figured, 'why bother saying "hi" or introducing yourself to people you don't know. Eventually you're just going to leave again, just do what you can but do not get close to anyone. That's how you're going to get hurt and you know it, so stay away.'

Once he came to his senses, he sat down and waited for the female bartender, who was too busy flirting with a fat man who seemed, from his accent, to be from Alabama.

He had been to Alabama once... it did not go well.

All he could think in his mind was, "Ignorant Racist Sons of bitches," so he made sure that his seat was far away from someone like that.

"Come on now, Sug, just a quick one on the lips and I promise I'll leave ya to ya work," belched the fat man.

That turned the bartender off immediately, and she handed him the bill stating, "Ya'll don't come back now, ya hear?" She moved on now to the new patron who joined her bar.

"Howdy Hun, what can I get you?" she asked. The man replied, "Black Tooth Grin on the rocks."

"Now that there's a man's drink sir!" the fat man retorted back. He was ignored by both people.

"Black Tooth Grin? Umm, I've never heard of that drink," she said, disappointed. "Did you make that drink up?" she asked back, hoping she could try and save her disposition as a bartender.

"Just pour in some crown and coke and wait for the drink to turn black," replied the man. He was unfortunately disappointed.

For someone who sported a Pantera t-shirt in a sports bar as a bartender, you would think she would know about the members of the former band and their likes. But then again, maybe he was the one obsessed with one of his favorite heavy metal bands.

The bartender did exactly as she was told and returned with his drink. "I've never heard of this drink before, but it looks yummy though." The man just smiled and took a sip of his black tooth. "So, where you from Hun?" she asked curiously. It was like the drink intrigued her to learn more about this stranger.

"Sorry, I'm afraid I'm not allowed to say," said the man.

That did it. Immediately, the bartender pulled up a chair from behind and sat right across from him, the only thing separating her from getting too close to him was the bar top. "Now You Gotta Tell Me!!!" she said excitedly yet flirtatiously.

The man knew already he was about to get cornered into a trap like a rat, and unless he was going to be an asshole like he usually was and pay and leave her there with that puppy dog look in her eyes, he couldn't be rude to her.

"Alright," he started, "I'm from Canada. I'm actually a farmer and I just thought it would be nice to come down to Texas just to see what the farming situation was like down here."

The bartender looked at him with some hint of skepticism, but nonetheless asked for more about him.

"After seeing how things are like here in Houston, I think I might take my business elsewhere. Nothing personal, but I feel that if you really want to make a living as a farmer, you also have to be comfortable with where you're gonna be living as well. Now Texas has its hospitable spots, but at least in Canada the temperature is a little more dryer up there than it is here. I'm the type of person who prefers a dry environment over one that's always humid and muggy. To me there's a difference between dry and humid. Dry means that the land you're on is still hospitable to live and eat off of, you'll be able to make a living enjoying the temperature. Humid means that you sweat more than a pregnant sow, and every time you walk your ass drips another ten gallons of sweat. The ground may be dry, but it's definitely not livable by any means necessary."

At the words "Ass drip" and "ten gallons," the bartender let out a chuckle and started to move closer towards the man. If she had been any closer, her breasts would be careening over the bar top.

The man thought in his head, 'She's cute, especially if she's a rocker. Maybe I could spend a couple of days here in Houston before I leave.' A small smirk came across his face, and that just made her smile even bigger.

"NOW SEE HEEYA SON!!!" said a very agitated voice. The man suddenly felt a very heavy palm set down on his left shoulder.

At once, the feelings of anger and death filled his brain. The man clearly did not like to be touched.

"You are one of the stupidest, lyin' sacks of shit I've ever had the opportunity of meeting. Anyone who's brighter than a five-year-old knows that Canada is all cold and full a' snow and shit, so I ask you now, where are these dry climates you talkin' 'bout?!!" said the fat man.

"Uh sir, I believe this man would like to have a drink alone, so would you mind not swearing in this establishment, or I'm going to ask you to leave!" replied the courageous yet scared shitless of his size bartender.

"Shut your face bitch!!! Or I'll smack it so hard ya momma won't even recognize what a cunt of a daughter she has," retorted the fat man.

By this point, the only thing that this quiet man could think of was how to make this guy hurt... bad!!! He quietly sipped his black tooth one more time and responded back in a very patient but dangerous voice.

"Take your Goddamn hand off of me and watch your mouth, or I promise you I will fuck you up!"

Fatty wasn't intimidated. "Boy, do you know who you're dealing wi...." the last word didn't quite come out because the quiet man, with a very swift smack with his right hand, had caught the Alabaman right in the fat man's temple, knocking him completely unconscious.

Luckily and fortunately for the quiet man, he was able to carry the overweight Alabaman and place him on the chair where the quiet man was sitting before. It happened so quickly that hardly anyone noticed.

All except the bartender, who was now standing with her jaw wide open.

The man wasn't sure if she was going to call security or just scream, people who get in trouble at airports usually don't get let off too leniently.

"How the hell did you do that?" the bartender asked.

"Attention all passengers: Flight 1080 with nonstop travel to Los Angeles is now preparing to board. Please make your way to the gate at this time," was the message from the intercom. The man gulped his drink and paid with a $50 bill so that the female bartender would keep quiet.

"Have a nice day," he said as he turned to leave.

"WAIT!!!" she replied. He turned around and waited to hear "Security" being screamed, only to have, "What's your name?" being asked. The man looked at her for five seconds and responded:

"Name's D, and I have a flight to catch." He turned and walked away; the bartender looked upon him and then at the fat man who lay drooling on the bar table. "Ugh!!! Why?" was what she said.

CHAPTER 2
Los Angeles – LAX Airport

The heat was more unbearable than it was back in Texas. Almost as soon as D stepped off of the plane, his shirt was already sticking to his chest due to all of the sweat.

He reached into his bag of candy and realized with an expression of half annoyance and sadness that he had eaten all of the sour patch. Was it really that long of a flight?

D made his way towards a small group of security officials. One of them looked up from his coffee and eyed D very suspiciously, then noticed a badge hanging off of his duffle bag.

"So, you're the Texan? You don't look like much, and here they were telling me you're this big guy with brawns for brains, shit you look like someone only a mother could love." He started to laugh so hard his face started to turn red after five seconds.

D had the right mind to just punch him in the face, but was afraid that he would lose his hand underneath all of that lard that he called a face.

"Where are your boots, Crockett?" said the officer. Apparently it was customary for people from out of Texas to give Texans a big hassle. D just smiled and said in a sarcastic hic accent:

"Well I tell you what Pardner, I just knew that somewhere here in this fine state of Cali-for-ni-a there was gonna be one asshole who was gon' be checkin' other people's feet because he wishes that someday his fat sloppy, lazy sack o' shit of an ass would love the feeling of having his hands pull hard on a fine piece of leather boots that would cut off his circulation so quick, the doctor wouldn't have time to declare him a diabetic because the poor fuck's leg would already be gone... so I left them at home because I knew there's always gotta be one."

At that, the officer stopped laughing and just stood there with his mouth so wide open that a fly was able to make its way into his mouth.

"Now, if you'll be so kind as to direct me to Captain Overstreet, and I'll be on my way," D said.

The officers just looked at each other and turned to a door that led towards another outside area that was off limits to all civilians.

D, however, was no civilian.

At thirty-seven years old, he was in peak condition; having trained with various martial artists from different countries and studied different languages to help him get around. True, he was a Texan, but many years of moving around after his parents were killed only caused him to move around a lot from one state to the other and, at some point in time, one country to the other. He was never a stickler for the rules set before him. He could never conform to authority because he felt that those in a position of authority, minus a few, only got where they were at because of too much ass kissing and sleeping around.

Surprisingly though, D, whose real name was Darrell Ford, succumbed to the intimidating presence of his superior, Captain Overstreet.

He strode past the officers with a smug look on his face and through the door. It led outside to where the landing strip was, and he saw four uniformed individuals talking amongst each other.

One was pinned up so tight with medals on his uniform one would think he was a walking Christmas ornament for the US military; he was a captain by the looks of his stripes. The others were just soldiers awaiting orders for their next assignment.

"That'll be all, gentlemen, dismissed!" said Overstreet. The soldiers saluted and ran towards one of the plane hangars that D did not recognize but did not question or did not care.

D walked up to Overstreet; his demeanor automatically changed as soon as he approached his former commander. The captain turned around and gave a big hearty smile, "Ford!!!" he cried. "You crazy Fuck!!! How've you been?" He walked up and hugged D, which he returned only half-heartedly.

"It's been a while, Captain, so tell me why I had to leave Texas during summer break at Galveston to come all the way to California," said D.

Overstreet just chuckled and replied, "Galveston?! Hell Ford, I thought you out of all people would hit up South Padre. More Mexican women there than meets the eye that would be willing to blow you the minute you glance at them. Plus, Galveston is nasty. You call that paradise?!!"

Captain Overstreet, whose real name was Jonathan, was a decorated man. He had seen many tragedies and deaths during his time on the battlefield, including friends and relatives. Yet despite having survived death plenty of times, he was still able to maintain his composure and still hand out a good chuckle or joke every now and then. He was two years older than D, and most people would consider them brothers. They had met when D was stationed in Afghanistan, D having taken a bullet in the chest to protect him from an enemy sniper's fire.

How D knew there was a sniper in the area, Overstreet would never know. All he remembers was that the wound was pretty deep, and that D was sure to die that day. By some miracle though, or God taking pity on his dumbass, D survived to tell the tale... if he wanted. Since then, Overstreet has always had a great respect for D because of his selfless duty to help others and has always insisted that D refer to him by his first name.

D, however, was not without respect either and knew how

to address his superiors.

"You know me, Captain, I prefer more quiet waters. I prefer places that allow me to breathe rather than get nose deep in a bunch of teenager's personal crap... fuckin kids," D said.

Captain Overstreet knew D too well, and though D would say derogative obscenities about children or worse... teenagers, he still saw a soft side in his former student's personality. Especially when D saved a newborn baby from the garbage when his mother dumped him there. Of course, all of that happened before D went up to both "parents," beat the living shit out of the father and cursed the mother out so badly that she might need some psychological evaluation. When asked how he found the parents in the first place, he would just reply, "None of your business!!!"

"Just remember that you used to be one, Darrell, so don't be too hard on 'em... anyways, the reason I called you here is because I'm giving you a different kind of assignment. Now I know you've always said that you wanted to visit Australia and I think I might have just the thing for you. There seems to be a bit of trouble happening around the Northern Territory, about an hour and a half away from Darwin."

Although D did seem interested in what he was talking about, he didn't show it. That was just the way he was, though; he was too busy staring at some birds that landed right in front of one of the runways.

"Am I boring you?" said Overstreet very curtly. D then turned back to him and replied, "Nope!"

"As I was saying, we have received reports of some suspicious activity happening near Jabiru. It's a little town situated near the Ranger Uranium Mine four miles away, or as they like to say, 6.4 kilometers. Apparently, some workers have been found murdered, plus there have been rumors of radiation sickness in the area. What astounds me the most is... well, the cause of death was very... interesting."

D finally turned his attention towards the captain and

asked, "Interesting how?" The captain continued to walk with D a little bit further towards a hangar labeled 'Property of the US MILITARY: OFF LIMITS TO ALL CIVILIANS.'

He stopped right in front of the building and replied, "The manner in which they were found and murdered. Your job is to investigate the murders, find a loophole or anything that could fit any pattern relating to everything happening in the area and stop it from continuing."

He then pointed to a cargo plane carrying what looked like medical supplies. The men entering the aircraft looked very stern and did not even look or glance in anyone's direction but on their work. D knew it was because they were trained to just "follow orders" and fuck everything else. Yet something about these men made D a little nervous, which was very rare as D was not intimidated very easily.

Seeing as though he was about to board a plane with these people, he felt he could justify why he was timid.

As he collected his belongings, he turned back to his mentor and asked, "How long will I be in Australia... a week, a month?"

Overstreet pondered this question for a moment and replied, "That's up to you."

Rather than ask more questions about where he was going and get annoyed, D boarded the plane. Once inside, he strapped himself into one of the seats that most military men use to travel and pulled out some headphones.

One of the men saw him and asked, "First time to the outback?" D nodded and slipped one of the headphones into his right ear. The man continued to stare and said, "Nice knowing you," before walking away off the ramp of the plane.

D had been intimidated by strangers before, so that's why he did not respond. Instead he placed the other headphone in his ear and closed his eyes as he listened to the iPhone that was in his front pouch. He didn't even feel the plane take off.

CHAPTER 3
JABIRU AIRPORT

The time difference was normal for D. Adjusting to time in different parts of the world had to be part of his everyday life. Otherwise, he knew it would kill him later.

As he got off the plane, he headed straight towards a jeep that was parked right next to a gas station within the airport grounds. The jeep doors read Kakadu National Park with a man dressed in safari attire and a cowboy hat. Normally D would just walk the other way and find his own means of transportation, but the man was holding a sign with his name on it.

"Your name is Ford? Darrell Ford?" D nodded and shook the man's hand.

"Yes sir," he replied.

"Name's Roger, mate. I've been assigned to lead and guide you throughout ya stay 'ere in good ol' Jabiru," he replied.

D only gave a little smile and entered into the man's small jeep. By the looks of what he saw inside, D assumed the man was a nerd. There were robot dogs from Japan strewn about the floor of the jeep and different sorts of metal that hung off behind the car. On the dashboard, D saw a hula girl who stayed motionless in the windless heat that was Australia.

Roger entered into the driver's side and attempted to start the car. Unfortunately, because it was an old, dilapidated vehicle, there was no such luck.

"Damn bloody thing's always fuckin' around. A good kick

in her good parts oughta do it," he said as he exited the vehicle and went straight to the hood of the car.

It was more than just a "kick." D watched in both amusement and surprise as this middle-aged man got on top of the actual engine and started jumping on it, screaming and begging for the damn thing to start. "C'mon now Sheila, there's a good girl.... WORK YOU BLASTED OL' BAG!!!"

By now everyone on the airstrip turned their heads to see a man jumping on the car, and another man in the passenger seat with his head in one of his hands just shaking his head and laughing under his breath.

D, however, had enough after about five minutes and moved into the driver's side to turn the key halfway. There was the answer.

D got out of the car and walked over to Roger, who was still screaming and acting like one of the local aborigines with his balls cut off.

"Hey bud?" D said.

Roger stopped what he was doing and turned with a smile on his face as if nothing had ever happened. "Yea mate, what can I do for ya?" he replied.

D smiled back and asked him to come down... calmly. Then he walked Roger over to the driver's side and pointed to the dashboard, where an orange sign with a gas station symbol kept blinking on and off.

Roger just stared for about ten seconds, then looked around. Everyone was just staring right back. He collected himself and then said, "Well now, looks like we need gas!"

D was trying his best not to say something rude and disrespectful, he felt bad for the guy. It really did seem like the man did not have many friends and only acted this way to try and help others out. However, in this case, it was a little extreme.

D just walked over to the passenger side and got in; Roger followed into the driver's side.

*

The heat became more intense, more than it was back in Texas. This time D could feel the sweat all over, it was intolerable. Roger was sweating too from his forehead. He removed his cowboy hat and wiped the water from his already balding cranium. He reached into the back and pulled out a canteen, took a big swig and handed it to D. D took it and drank... five seconds later he spat all over the dashboard.

"Whisky?" D said. "You have whisky in your canteen?"

Roger just shrugged and took the canteen and drank again. "Calms the nerves mate, especially on a hot day," he replied.

"One would think to drink a lot of water in this case, but you take the cake," D laughed. When he looked at Roger, the man still looked bummed out, almost embarrassed. "Dude, you're not still upset about the car, are you?" D said.

Roger reacted quickly. "Car? What? Oh that, naw, is all good mate. Happens all the time."

D just nodded his head and looked out the topless car. He expected to see desert terrain with kangaroos hopping around. Instead, he was surprised to see more marshland than anything else, with lots of birds flying about. He could smell nature all around him. It reminded him of Texas so much.

He propped his black tactical boots on top of the panel of the car and raised up his own black cowboy hat he had stashed away. "How long have you been working at the park, Rog?" he asked.

D was glad to see that Roger had chilled out a bit and started to talk a little more casually. "Well, I've been in the region for all my life, born and bred. I used to work with my father on a lot of the land that you see around you. Technically, this is my property."

D looked around again and just whistled. "You must have a lot under your name, your own land? Makes me kind of envious, having your own land and all."

"You would think that, right?" Roger said.

It wasn't a rude answer. It was more 'matter of fact.'

D turned his head towards him and inquired, "What makes you say that?"

Roger paused for a bit, then asked D a question that caught him off guard. "Do you believe in ghosts, mate?"

D just stared. Very unusual question seeing as how they had just barely met.

"Never met or seen one," D said proudly. "Then again, I don't believe in any of that junk."

Roger continued on. "Well, do you believe in God?"

"I am a Christian. Yes, I do believe and accept. But ghosts and paranormal crap of that sort... nah!" D stated.

"Mate, if you believe in God, you have to believe in some sort of afterlife," Roger said. "The only reason I bring it up is because I think my park and property might be haunted."

D listened but stood by his answer and beliefs. "Like I said, I've never seen anything of that sort. I've heard stories, yes, but I believe in the saying from the bible. 'Seeing is Believing.' If I can't see it, I don't believe it."

"Well, I think you might change your mind while you're here," Roger said. "A lot of crazy shit has been happenin' lately around here."

Since it was his job, he had to ask. "Like?" D inquired.

"Where to start? Crazy lights shinin' within the center of Kakadu. Animal carcasses strewn about the place. Mysterious figures walking around at night. Lots more if you want to know later on," Roger explained.

"Pass," D said. "Unless it has something to do with terroristic threats or humanity in danger. It. Can. Wait."

To him, there was always a logical explanation for everything.

Deep inside though, even though D was a Christian, he knew that he wasn't a very good Christian. Sure, he believed in God, but most of D's decisions and actions in life made him question whether he was who he said he was.

Then again, all of his close calls with death might have been because he was 'saved' by a mysterious presence in his life. D should be dead. He figured though, that since he was alive, God was the reason for it.

"Maybe it is terroristic," Roger said.

D chuckled. "I doubt it, but OK," he said.

"Now think about it. I did say that there were mysterious lights in the park," Roger countered.

D replied. "Swamp gas, or maybe you have looters that come into the park to fuck around."

"OK, the animal carcasses?" Roger pressed on.

"It's Australia, Roger, just like in Texas, animals eat each other for survival. That's always the logical explanation," D said.

Roger was having a difficult time explaining, but he presented it anyway. "Mysterious figures?" he asked.

D took a huge breath and answered. "Like I said. You've got looters or teenagers that are yanking your chain. Do you have security at the park?"

"Oh sure, Todd is his name. Very nice guy!" Roger said.

"I would really get him to 'do his job.' Once he finds your looters, your problem is solved," D said.

Roger realized he was not going to get anywhere with his new companion.

He turned his head towards D and asked, "What part of Texas are you from, mate?"

D stayed quiet, then responded, "Don't know. I really don't know where I was born. I moved around a lot when I was young, but a majority of it has always been in Texas. It wasn't until I enlisted in the Marines that I started to see places I've never been before."

"Well, where are your parents?" Roger asked.

When, after ten seconds, he didn't hear an answer to his question, he knew he struck a nerve. Roger immediately started to feel like crap again. "Sorry mate, I know it's none of my business," he said.

D just stared out the window and continued to look at all the wetlands that surrounded him and his new... 'co-worker.' "Any crocs around these parts? I've never seen one in the wild before, especially in another country. Sorry, I am a bit of an animal enthusiast," D said.

Roger then started to explain about all the different wildlife that ranged in the Northern Territory: flocks of budgerigars and parrots, wild horses and buffalo, "Even wombats, dingoes, lions, tigers, and monkeys," Roger said with great enthusiasm. "Of course, the lions, tigers and monkeys are all at the park, so... ya more than welcome to come out and see it. Free of charge!"

D was glad that they changed the subject, any more awkwardness from the two of them and he might have to yell.

CHAPTER 4

The Smithston Uranium Mine was just dead ahead. It looked exactly like a pit that D remembered back in Arizona, except much bigger.

D saw the factory where all the workers would experiment and research all of the ores and try to extract all of the uranium that lay within it. His attention, however, was strictly towards what was mutilating all the workers.

He had heard stories from Overstreet about how the mine had several accusations of safety breaches, some even involving radioactive water from spilling into the wetlands of where Roger worked, Kakadu National Park. The most recent incident was back in 2013 when a tank burst open and the factory had to be shut down.

With D calculating all of the problems being associated with the plant, he guessed that the causes of death were mostly due to clumsiness rather than any faulty mechanisms.

The chief supervisor onsite approached D and Roger; the Texan was annoyed... again.

The man approached them with much arrogance and a very unfriendly vibe to anyone that he didn't know. He was also obese, VERY obese. This man clearly did not take care of himself as there were food and beverage stains all along his shirt. He had thin black hair and sunken eyes, but the rest of his face was just plump. D was afraid that if he took a needle and poked his belly, lard would spray out. The way he approached them too, was pretty pathetic. It was more of a waddle.

"You again?!" the rude bastard said; he was obviously aware of how many times Roger had come to visit them.

Usually, it was because of the pollution that was coming into the park from the mine, so Roger was trying his best to keep them at bay most of the time. This time, however, he had another good reason to be there.

"G'day Murray, hope all's well. I brought the Yank I was tellin' you 'bout. Ya know, the one from Texas?" Roger replied.

D stepped forward and presented his hand in respect to shake. Murray just took one look at it and looked right back at D, clearly not interested in visitors or tourists.

"Yea, I'm aware of this bloke, but I told you and the rest of the bloody Americans who have come by here that all is well, and we don't take kindly to people who don't belong here," said Murray.

By the term "bloody Americans," D only thought about Overstreet and all the other military officials who had come by the plant, but D didn't care. He spoke his mind.

"Well, first of all, I didn't ask to be here, and second, I don't give a shit if your stupid ass claims 'all is well.' I'm here to do a job and find out why your workers are getting killed. Now, if all was well, you wouldn't be in this situation right now, and I wouldn't have been bothered from my island paradise in Galveston to be here to help you. So do me and the rest of society a favor and shut your fat fuckin' mouth before someone ends up shutting it for you, CAPICE?" retorted D sternly.

Roger looked as if he was about to faint from the tone and foul language that the "Yank" was using. D looked as if he was ready to kill someone. Murray just stood there with his mouth open and a little bit of drool coming down. He looked uncomfortable, if not scared.

He collected himself and cleared his throat before saying, "I see, my apologies. I had no idea that Americans were so angry a majority of the time and willing to start fights when they saw fit."

D was prepared for a comeback. "No, we only hurt the stupid, fat, arrogant ones who don't know their ass from their pie hole they call a mouth!" he shot back.

It was a good thing Roger finally stepped in before blood was spilled.

"Alright, Alright! Let's just get on with it then. Why don't you show him where the incidents have been takin' place Murray."

Murray took the both of them inside the pit, with one of the golf carts they used to get around from place to place. As D looked around, he could see that a lot of the workers looked miserable, probably overworked. The atmosphere seemed gloomy and depressing as well, compared to outside. There was oil all over the place and bits of rock and dirt strewn about on the machines and equipment. Typical working environment, but the workers didn't seem to be paying any attention at all.

If anything, D noticed that they kept looking at their watches. Waiting to clock out. All heads turned to the new visitor from America, they were all very curious. Then it came to him, these workers had never seen a person from another country before. This was all new to them.

As they drove deeper into the mine, D started to notice that the lights become dimmer. Some of the light bulbs had shorted out and were never replaced. Not that it mattered, there were no workers in the area, so no complaints.

There was something else that D could sense: the smell and walls. There was a foul odor in the air, almost as if someone died and no one claimed the body. The walls looked like slime was pouring out of them. He assumed that it was oil though from the mine, but as he looked closer, he noticed that the slime was red.

"Murray, what is this stuff on the walls?" D asked.

Murray took one glance at the walls and stopped the car. He stepped out and touched the slime with two fingers, then brought them to his nose. As he sniffed, he coughed and gagged a bit.

D got out of the car and looked closely at the slime, but did not touch it. Funny, it was almost as if it were the slime from a movie he once saw back in the 80s, but D knew better than to touch something that he was not aware of.

"Blimey! What in the flyin' fuck is this stuff, and why does it smell so bad?!" Murray demanded, as if D knew the answer already. D got up and reached into his duffel bag's compartments and pulled out a pen. He then went up to the slime and scooped a bit on the pen. Roger shined a flashlight on the substance and noticed that the light seemed to have an effect on it. The once red goo now turned pale, it was as if it were camouflaged.

D turned to Murray and said, "You tell me, it seems as if this stuff has been down here for quite some time."

"Well, I certainly didn't put it here!" he retorted.

"I didn't say you did," D responded, as if Murray was already guilty of something. "How far until we get to the area where the men were killed?" he asked Roger. He wouldn't have got anywhere if he had asked Murray. It was a waste of time.

"Well, we're standin' in it," Roger said.

D looked around with the flashlight he took from Roger and noticed the ground.

Footprints, but not from him or the others. Instead, the prints had toes, they were very big.

D stood up once again and said, "Either Bigfoot followed me from America, or you all have one huge motherfucker working in this mine... just saying."

Murray looked like he might erupt and Roger, with a huge smile on his face, was clearly excited.

"Well, I'll be, a bloody Sasquatch! This is incredible, this is great...."

"You're both fuckin' looney!" interrupted Murray, who was now red with anger. He marched right over to where D stood.

D was ready for a fight if need be. He was not in the mood for stupidity.

Murray took one look at the print, examined it carefully and then said, "Damn workers, always playin' tricks. Have they no respect for the dead?!"

He then kicked the dirt that the print was in. "I told both of you this was a waste of time. You Americans think that you know more than any other country in this world, well you're wrong! We know how to take care of our own around here, and we know the bush a lot better than some bloody Yank who thinks a Bigfoot is running amok in our mine!"

Murray was burning red and out of breath. Any further, and he was liable for a heart attack. D pressed on anyway.

"Are you done being an asshole?" he said calmly.

Before Murray had a chance to react, there was a scream coming from further into the mine.

All three got quickly into the cart and zoomed towards the area.

When they got there, no light was present at all and, to make things stranger, everything was now deadly silent.

D quietly got out of the cart and turned on the flashlight. He turned to the other two and asked quietly, "You two coming?"

Roger looked terrified, and Murray just replied, "Hell No! You're the one they hired, so have at it."

It was official, D was going to beat the living crap out of him later, not because he was a jerk but because he was hiding something. From the start, D knew that Murray seemed very agitated and withdrawn. He would get to the bottom of it later.

D walked into the darkness and felt very cold. He'd been in harsh climate conditions before, but this was different. He had been joking about the whole Sasquatch thing earlier, but now he was starting to wonder if this was really caused by some sort of serial killer or if this was something else... something not human.

The only sounds made were his boots crunching the dirt.

He noticed something up ahead that looked light colored.

As he got closer, he saw that it was a light brown work boot still attached to its human counterpart. D moved a little faster to check and see if the man was still alive, and then the light went out.

He thought to himself, 'Go figure that Roger wouldn't have checked the batteries, let alone the gas gauge for the jeep.'

He banged the light a couple of times before the light went back on in his face again. When he shined it where the boot was, it was gone.

'That's interesting,' D thought. As he walked further, he noticed more red matter. This time he knew it wasn't the slime from before. D knew all too well, after so many years of service in the military and where it took him, that this was human blood. Though it was a small puddle, he had to report it.

As he turned to go back to the cart, there stood a man who stared right into D's eyes.

D looked at the man and saw that he was in bad shape. The man's clothes were shredded to pieces, and there were bruises and deep cuts that needed immediate medical attention. What got him the most was the man's face. It was horribly mangled.

Vomit started to rise in D's throat. Most victims he saw were usually passed out from blood loss, but this guy acted as if he was in a trance.

"Hey! You alright? You're in shock. Just stay still and take deep, calm breaths, do you understand?" D said.

Though he thought it was stupid to ask a question like 'You alright?' He examined closer to the facial area and saw that the victim's lips were pretty much on the other side of his cheek than where a normal mouth should be.

The man replied in gurgles of his own blood and started to walk towards D. "OK, just stay right there, you need help." The man kept moving forward, ignoring D's command.

The man then raised his hands up, and D saw what should

have been ten fingers, instead were only six of them. They were lopped off but not cut. D looked closely from where he stood and noticed the little bit of clear liquid and then realized... they were chewed off.

"Don't move! You need to stay still!" commanded D, and that's when the man keeled over and lay very still. Clearly not fazed by what he saw, D walked forward and examined the body a little more carefully.

Being cautious not to touch it, he checked all over the body to see if there were any more bite marks or scratches.

From the looks of it, it was just another animal attack inside the mine that might be killing the workers. What stood out, though, was the man's head. He moved closer with the flashlight to see the damage.

There was grey matter sticking out of a crack in the back of the man's skull, and then he noticed indentations on the sides of his head.

D automatically saw that they were finger marks. What kind of animal could crush a man's head without the use of its jaws?

There was scuffling behind D, and he turned to see Roger and Murray both looking terrified. "My... God...," Murray said as he walked closer.

"Yea, 'all is well,' isn't it Murray? Tell me, is this your definition of 'all is well', or are you really just dumb not to know what's going on?" D retorted.

"The hell you talkin' 'bout?!!, I didn't want this for the bastard, and again, this is what we called you down here for, isn't it?!!" Murray replied angrily.

D stood his ground and said sarcastically, "I thought you didn't need help from 'bloody Americans.'"

Roger knelt down near the body, clearly shaken but nonetheless concerned about who the victim was.

He pulled the man's wallet out and opened it up. Murray, watching this, said, "Oy, what are you doin'? Rob a man while he's dead, are you daft?"

Roger pulled out the man's ID and said, "His name was Oliver Gladstone; he was a father of four." He then showed his children in the pictures of the wallet. D felt a pinch in his heart and saw that from the looks on these kids' faces, they loved their father very much. Now they would never see him again. D knew the feeling but quickly brushed it away.

"Call an ambulance. We need to get his body outside," he spoke.

*

Up top, the authorities were making reports with Murray, who decided to take charge of the situation and inform them about what happened.

One particular detective gave notice to D's direction as Murray was speaking, then gave his attention back to the lard sack.

The cause of death was claimed to be a mining accident, that some workers were horsing around with a mine cart and it went off the tracks and crushed the man to death. What Murray did not tell the police was that the victim was still alive when D saw him. Of course, he didn't know the full story, but felt he didn't want D to say anything, otherwise his mine would be closed indefinitely until they got to the bottom of this.

D looked over to where Murray was giving the statement, and Roger walked over to him with his canteen again.

D took a drink and then squinted as if he just put a whole bunch of sour candies in his mouth. "Next time, warn me when you put rum in a canteen instead of whisky."

Roger smiled. "Sorry mate, just thought you could use some."

D smiled back. Roger was only trying to lighten the mood and, so far, he was the only one that D could rely on and talk with rationally and sanely. D could see though that Roger still looked unsettled and nervous.

"Talk to me Rog, you OK?" D asked.

Roger looked up and replied, "What really happened down there? We didn't hear from you for about ten minutes, and that's when we heard you talkin' to someone. He was still alive, wasn't he?"

D took another drink of rum before speaking and explained everything from top to bottom, then finished by saying, "Yea, he still was, though not for long. He was the one I was talking to right before he died."

Roger examined D closely and asked, "You're not at all shaken up by this? A man was just brutally murdered and you're just peachy. If you ask me, I'd be shittin' up peas and carrots for a lifetime."

"It's nothing that I haven't seen before. You'd be surprised by what I have seen. This was no different," D lied.

He looked at Roger, who was scratching his head. "Did you know the victim?" he asked.

"Yea, I knew him," replied Roger. "I knew him when he first started working here. He was a very nice boy, very respectful. So kind to Murray, though Murray was just a big ass to him. My God, he was going to be married next week."

At this moment, Roger took a drink of rum, and D just stood there taking in all that had happened that day. He felt sorry for Roger, who again had a very kind heart. It was the victim's family though that would be mourning the most.

Roger collected himself and asked, "You hungry?"

D looked at him, and Roger's smile faltered.

That's when D replied, "Yea, I am. What's to eat around here."

Roger's smile lit up again. "I know a great place around here, come on."

As D got into the jeep, he paused and looked over his shoulder. Roger paused too and watched. "Everythin' alright?" he asked.

"Thought I heard something. Never mind," D replied, and

as they sped off, a tall, dark figure moved quietly in the bushes where D looked before. It gave a grunt but ended with a hiss.
It then turned and walked away.

CHAPTER 5

LONE SMITHSTON ROAD – A FEW MILES OUTSIDE KAKADU NATIONAL PARK

"So, what's to eat around here? Whataburger, McDonalds, Pizza Hut... Taco P?" D asked.

Roger looked at his new friend as if he were an alien from another planet when he asked those questions.

"Um, mate, remember this is Australia. Your usual cuisine in America is not really that common here in the Northern Territory," said Roger.

D looked disappointed, but nevertheless waited to see where Roger was taking him. When they got there, D expected to see some sort of restaurant or shack off the side of the road.

Instead, he saw a farm, with sheep running along the front of the property, and an old dilapidated house with a huge barn in the back. In a way it reminded him of Texas.

"Well, here we are, home sweet home!" Roger said.

As soon as they got out of the jeep, two German Shepherds ran out to greet them. One of them automatically jumped on D like a child running to their mom or dad.

"Whoa there... ah... okay... down dog... down." D struggled with the dog until it was calm. That's when she lay on the ground and waited to be petted some more. D knelt and started to rub the dog's ears.

"Ah, she likes ya. You're very lucky. Most of the time she aims for the balls of someone she doesn't know. You should feel honored," Roger said and took both dogs by the collar.

D got up and asked, "This place is yours? Nice... at least

you have a home." The last part he mumbled to himself.

"You say somethin', mate?" Roger asked, but D changed the subject:

"So, what's for dinner?"

Roger opened the front door and let D in first. He felt like he was back in Texas.

The front of the house looked very decorated with home-made furniture made from the hides of cattle, a buffalo rug on the floor and different sorts of portraits and paintings on the wall. It would all look great if it weren't for all the clutter on the floor that D had to step over.

Once again, he saw different sorts of appliances lying around as if the whole house was just one big workshop: from hammers to saws, wrenches to different sorts of drivers.

Of course, D would have a problem with that. Aside from being the way he was, he was also a neat freak.

"Mind the mess, will ya? Haven't had a chance to clean the place in a while," Roger explained.

"In a while?" D said. "How long has it been since you've been here?"

Roger started to count his fingers from one to five, and then stated, "Two weeks! But don't worry, the dogs know where to find their food," Roger said.

That wasn't the point D was trying to get across, but fig-ured, don't be rude. It's not every day

that someone invites you into their home, most just say, 'Fuck you and the white horse you rode in on.'

D sat himself down on the couch while the female jumped up and started moving her head towards D's lap.

As he was petting her, D could hear Roger in the kitchen banging away and swearing to himself. D then closed his eyes and lay back for a while.

He tried not to think about what he had seen today, but it was imprinted into his mind.

The sight of that man in the tunnels, all mangled and bloody, made D feel a little uneasy as to what he might be walking into. As he thought to himself what it could have been that attacked him, his main thought was a bear or huge cat. But he was in Australia now and not America, so what animal could do that? In all the years he had seen murder and bloodshed, this one bothered him the most, and that annoyed him. D was not afraid of anything, so why was he all worked up?

"ORDER UP!!!" cried a voice very familiar to D, and he opened his eyes to see a plate of what looked like roast beef with mashed potatoes held right in front of him.

He took the plate with his left hand and realized that his right hand was placed on the handle of a bowie knife he kept in his holster. Years of fighting and being on guard at all times had made him on edge, and he didn't take new surroundings lightly.

However, his train of thought was lost once he smelled the food in front of him, and his mouth started to water.

"Well, don't wait for me, mate, dig in!" exclaimed Roger as he ran back into the kitchen to grab his plate, the dogs following him.

D sat up straight and adjusted himself, and with his fork, took a bite of the roast beef. The food pretty much melted in his mouth as to how good it tasted, then he tried the mashed potatoes. He was in Heaven, and it almost made him forget about a dirty, smelly house. D couldn't remember when he last had a home-cooked meal, but he was grateful.

Roger returned with his plate only to see that D had pretty much finished half of his already. "Blimey!" he said. "Well, there's plenty more if you'd like. Maybe I should take up the career of a chef after all."

D replied, "You have my approval!" as he took another bite of beef and potato.

Roger looked satisfied for the first time that day; he had been trying to please D all day. "Well, now that I have you where I want, let me go ahead and say that you're more than welcome to stay here until the lads finish up your lodgings elsewhere," Roger said. "I've got a spare room in the back over here. Bed is a bit cheap, but it does the job."

D looked up from his meal and said, "Thanks, I wouldn't mind at all. The plane trip was a bit crappy."

As both of them finished their meal, Roger went back to the kitchen to make some tea to settle the stomach, with, of course, a splash of scotch to go with it.

D settled himself again into the couch while Roger made himself comfortable on a recliner. D started to ease up a bit now and started to chat with Roger about his time in the service as well as where he traveled during his employment with the US Government. When Roger asked about how he got involved with the government and why he was where he was at the time, D just said that it was classified, and Roger asked no more.

D couldn't quite give him all the details as that would terrify the living daylights out of him. He changed the subject, however. "So, what's with all the appliances, robot dogs and tools? You making something or fixing something?" D asked.

Roger sat up straight and replied, "Well... I am sort of an inventor. It's a hobby of mine when I'm not working at the preserve, I like to come up with all sorts of neat gadgets. Guess you could say I'm like your Batman back in America, just... a little bit older."

D was intrigued and asked, "What sorts of gadgets?"

That did it! Roger jumped from his seat and ran to another room, probably his bedroom. D heard clanging and banging again and had to roll his eyes. It seemed wherever Roger went off to, there was always going to be clanging and banging.

Roger returned with a handheld gadget that was attached to his right hand. It was connected to the bullet harness around his body. It almost looked like a sci-fi zapper from one of those 50s/60s movies, but in bracelet form. He, however, looked like an aged Rambo.

Roger showed it to D. "What do you think?"

D looked for about five seconds before replying, "Looks fabulous, looks awesome, looks great, grand, wonderful.... What is it?"

Roger's smile turned to a look of 'I should've known that was coming.' He then said, "Well, it may look like a video game zapper that these kids nowadays are playin' on, but I improved on it."

He then motioned for D to follow him outside to a barn... or what was left of a barn.

Sure, the structure still stood, but there were scorch marks and the smell of burnt wood inhabited the area. D also noticed small holes in the sides of the barn and knew all too well that they were bullet holes. Funny, Roger didn't carry any firearms in the house from what D saw.

"Now that I have you," Roger said, "you are the first to see my new product in action." He further explained, "Imagine, if you may, that you are in a tight area, with no way out.... I mean it, no doors or anythin' of that matter, but you need to get out."

He then walked toward the barn and aimed his bracelet at the side. With a push of a trigger in his thumb area, a barrage of bullets came flying out and started to destroy more of the barn.

D looked on in astonishment, but noticed that the bullets stopped. He then turned to look at Roger, who was on the floor laughing.

"I've basically made a handheld machine gun, and once you've shot enough holes in the area you're lookin' at, you can just smash your way through," he said.

He got up off the floor, turned to D excitedly and asked, "Well, what do you think?"

D was impressed, he wasn't going to lie, but there was one small problem.

"What happens if you're out of bullets?" D asked.

Roger just looked at D as if he was the stupidest person in the world before saying, "Well then your right fucked, mate!" he replied angrily and stormed off back to the house.

D could've sworn he heard him mumble, 'Why the bloody hell didn't I think of that? How stupid can I be?'

He stood there for a moment looking at the barn and what the bracelet did to it and thought that it would be pretty cool if it could be modified to break apart stone and rock. After all, he was all alone out here in the outback. Then D looked up into the sky and saw all the stars shining in the night. It had been a while since he had seen that. The last time was in Texas, but he never got to be in the state for more than two days before being called into another mission.

He turned around and walked towards the house. Surprisingly, the door was still open.

The female German Shepherd stood there waiting for him, wagging her tail, and D rubbed her head before entering the house. The dog followed him all the way into the living room as D wondered where he should sleep.

Feeling like he pissed Roger off, he figured don't bother asking him, so he lay down on the couch and relaxed a bit. He started to think about his time in Houston and how that one female bartender caught his eye and attention, but he knew it would never work out as he was always on the go.

He turned his head and saw the German Shepherd just staring at him. "What's up?" D said, and the dog just lowered herself onto the floor underneath D and lay down.

"Me too, girl..." He looked at the dog carefully before saying, "Me too."

He lay back again and closed his eyes, and started thinking again about why he had to be such an ass to people he just met. Before he knew it though, he was sound asleep.

He was overlooking a scene where two forms were standing on top of a bridge. From the looks of it, he thought maybe it was a scene from the Temple of Doom right before Indy cut down the ropes holding everything in place. He looked around and saw that they were being watched by eyes he did not recognize at all. It made him uncomfortable, but at the same time he knew the eyes weren't threatening. It was almost as if they were worried, wondering what was going to happen to the figures. He looked as the figure in front of him kept making eye contact with the other. What piqued his curiosity was that he knew they were human figures, but they were both different colors. One was large with bluish-white, while the other was small with pure black surrounding it. The bluish figure turned around and looked directly into his eyes; he could have sworn that he saw it smile. That's when he saw a black rod erupt from blue's chest, and that's when he heard screams all around. Blue fell to the bridge floor as the black form stood over him with its "sword," then it glanced into his eyes. The last thing he remembered was hearing, "I'm sorry," before everything went dark.

CHAPTER 6

Everything was pitch black, and it still felt like he was in the dream. It wasn't until he pulled on one of his eyelashes that he realized he was awake.

D sat up from the couch and pondered for a bit, the same dream over and over again. Out of all the dreams that have crept up into his mind at night, this one was the one that got his curiosity rolling the most.

He heard scuffling and looked to the floor to see the female German Shepherd lying at the foot of the couch. At least she kept you company despite how you acted last night, D thought.

He got up from the couch and walked toward the back door. He needed fresh air.

The sky at night in Australia looked so clear, the stars were as pure and clear as diamonds. The air smelled fresh too, Texas fresh. The good old days seemed to be the best for D,

back to a time when he actually felt at home and, out of all things... wanted.

Growing up wasn't easy for him, especially since he had no stable parental figure to guide him out of it. Moving from foster parent to foster parent, they all said the same thing: "He's a fucking crazy kid!" As a kid, D was always looking for a fight and, the majority of the time, got what he wanted. He remembered when some kid that he was living with at the time started to take other kids' meals without their consent. Once he got to D and tried to take his food, D took the kid's hand and smashed a meat pounder on it. After that, D had to go to some psychological classes for evaluation, but at least no one ever messed with his stuff again.

Wasn't his fault that he had no direction in life, or someone to show him how to get there. At least he did what was necessary to graduate from high school, even if he was in the mid percentile. He seemed to be highly favored by his ROTC instructors. They always took the time to help him with his personal life and with his studies.

It was because of them that D took the route of the military, joining the Marines at eighteen and graduating at the top of his class. Then it was off to Kuwait in the Middle East during the 1990s when Iraq took control. Assigned by his superior, Overstreet, under direct orders from the President himself, D was assigned to a ghost brigade. The brigade was not known at all by anyone in the military and was under strict orders to not disclose any information to anyone, not even to loved ones. D didn't have any problems with that, there were no loved ones for him... just his brothers in the Marines, and that was depending on if he liked them or not. Despite this, they worked together. It was during those missions in the Middle East that D and his comrades saw things that no other person should see. God, he prayed that no one had to endure what they saw and went through. Just thinking about it brought back....

He came to his senses when he heard something near the barn. It almost sounded like moaning, as if someone were hurt.

D calmly got up and headed towards the barn, stepping as carefully as possible to not disturb anything and scare away whatever the sound was. As the moaning got louder, D listened more closely and heard what he thought were sniffles. As he got to a piece of wood that was big enough to be what was left of a door, he heard the voice much clearer.

"Stupid git, ya can't do anythin' right... no matter how hard you try, you always manage to fuck everythin' up!"

D knew that voice. "Roger?" he called.

A snort sounded off like a horse, and Roger started to get up very quickly. D took one look at him and was a little uncomfortable with what he saw. Roger looked as if he had just come back from a funeral. His eyes were puffy and red with tears still streaming down his face, and there was snot flowing down his nose.

"Um... if this is a bad time, I can come back later," D said.

"Bad time? Every time is a bad time for me mate," Roger replied. "What did I do wrong? Huh? What is wrong with me? All I wanted to do was to make a good impression on ya, and instead I look like a complete arse. I don't bloody show my shit to people all the time, simply because they wouldn't understand. Instead, they would call me a Prat for a man my age to be tinkling around with knick-knacks and toys from other countries and trying to make things that could benefit man or someone else. But NOOOOO, every single time I open my bloody trap, I always end up looking like a twat!" Roger spewed out.

D just stood there taking everything in, not saying anything but listening. He felt bad for Roger. All the guy wanted was to make friends.

He sniffed around and wrinkled his nose. "What is that?" D asked.

Roger looked down and replied, "I get gas when I cry... I can't help it."

Now D felt really bad and disgusted at the same time. "Are you for real, dude?!" he said, but then regretted his words immediately.

"I SAID I CAN'T BLOODY HELP IT. WHAT ELSE DO YOU WANT FROM ME? PLUG UP ME BUM AND GAS IT OUT ME MOUTH?!" Roger roared.

D shut his mouth and just stared. Roger collected himself and said, "I'm sorry, I didn't mean to yell. I'm just tired is all."

D took a few seconds before saying to Roger, "It's cool man, being in the Marines and special forces, you kind of get used to it. I didn't mean any disrespect tonight. Sometimes I just say things that rub people the wrong way."

"I know that," Roger replied. "I had a father who always spoke his mind every single time something didn't quite go right for him... usually, he took it out on me. A shame really, I was only seven at the time... you would've thought that fathers would have given more comfort and guidance during that time. Instead, it was all work and no play, even when I tried to show him some of the inventions I made in my spare time...." He got quiet.

D was nervous to ask him what had happened, but did so anyway. "What did your father do when you showed him?" D asked.

Roger was staring at the night sky; the stars were starting to get brighter. He took a breath and then started:

"He would take it away and destroy it, then he would find me and show me what he had done. 'YOU'LL NEVER GET ANYWHERE IN LIFE IF YOU KEEP MAKING RUBBISH LIKE THIS! EVERY TIME YOU MAKE SHIT LIKE THIS, I'LL DESTROY IT AND THEN I'LL DO THIS.'" Roger said as he imitated his father.

New tears were streaming down his cheeks again, and then that's when he closed his eyes and said, "He beat the living crap out of me, said no son of his was ever going to be a twat of an inventor while he was still alive. He tried to break my spirit, he tried so hard... but he didn't win. Eventually mother had gotten tired of his shit and told him to 'fuck off!' Oh...my father did not like that at all. He swung at my mum. Hit her square in the jaw. I didn't know what to do...I was just hiding behind a closet door...I just heard scuffling around and all. Both of them were fighting. Then I heard my mum scream out that if he ever came back she would kill him. I remember her coming up to me and telling me everything was going to be alright. Her mouth was covered in blood but she still reassured me that there was nothing wrong with what I wanted to do and that I don't need someone like him pushing me around. And it's true to this day. I still make inventions and will continue to do so as long as I live. I showed him! I showed him good!"

D looked at this middle-aged, balding man. It was almost like staring at a rebellious teenager who wanted to break free from a society that 'just didn't understand the youth of these days.'

The man was obviously drunk. D discovered a bottle of wine on the ground. Either way, D saw a small smile form on Roger's mouth.

This man was quite accepting of how he was and what he did for a living, but at the same time still sought the approval of another figure who could relate as well.

"Then that's all that matters, Rog," said D. "You don't need someone else telling you that you're no good or that you won't amount to much because of your own personal choices."

Roger looked towards D as he continued, "That's what makes you the person you are, by how you want to be, not by what others want you to be."

Roger pondered a minute and then wiped the remaining tears off his face. "Fancy a drink, D?" Roger said.

D looked at him surprised and asked, "What did you call me?"

Roger said, "D! Sorry mate, I just thought it might be shorter to call you that. After all, you call me Rog."

D never told anyone what his nickname was, everyone always addressed him as 'Ford' or 'sir.' Nevertheless, it wasn't like anyone wouldn't think to use that name for him.

D changed his attitude and replied, "Drinks it is!" as both he and Roger headed back into his home, the dogs waiting for the two new friends at the entrance.

"Oh, by the way," D continued. "What's this beautiful girl's name?" he asked, referring to the female dog.

"Oh, that there is Sheila, very good girl! She definitely has taken a likin' to ya. Never seen her act like that before with anyone." Roger said.

D looked down at her and smiled. She returned by panting and jumping up on him, wanting to give him kisses. Not only did D make a new human friend, but he made his first animal friend as well. Life was good at the moment for D and Roger as the older gentleman reached into his liquor cabinet while D sat down with Sheila.

D paused in thought. "Wait, isn't your car named 'Sheila' as well?" D asked Roger.

Roger turned to D and replied. "Don't be hatin' on that name. I like it! Might as well name everyone 'Sheila.'"

He grinned and reached back into the liquor cabinet.

CHAPTER 7

Morning sucked.

It felt like D hadn't slept in days, and he had a very bad migraine, a hangover.

D stared straight at the ceiling and blinked a couple of times before registering where he was.

He remembered coming back into the house with Roger, downing a bottle of aged scotch that Roger kept in his study and listening to an old record player that was still playing what sounded like an Irish reel that just kept looping over and over again.

As he got up from the couch, the pounding in his head increased with such intensity that he had to sit back down. Closing his eyes, he concentrated on the one thing that always helped him in a situation like this: paradise.

Not a particular paradise, but one that he envisioned from time to time.

In his mind, there was a crystal-clear beach with calm tides swishing back and forth, followed by plenty of palm trees that stretched along the beach line with plenty of fruit and coconuts to keep him satisfied. And lastly, a hammock where he could rest and drown out everything that irked him. The funny thing is, he always believed in his mind that such a place existed and dreamed of one day retiring there and not having to worry about his past life or the mistakes he had made. As he thought about the waves silently moving back and forth, he then felt the presence of another person near him. In his thoughts, he opened his eyes and saw a beautiful woman standing over him, smiling. He smiled back and asked her, "Howdy ma'am, what brings you to my humble abode lovely?" She leaned over closer to him, and D closed his eyes, believing that he was going to get a big surprise.... That's when he heard, "YOURS?!! I LIVE HERE!!!" she said in an old cranky Australian accent.

D awoke from his dream, and right in front of him was Roger.

D let out a yelp that was close to the way Homer Simpson would freak out over something that scared him.

Roger backed up as well, clearly frightened. "Bloody Hell!!! What's got into ya?!! Next thing ya know you're gonna sputter all over me pillows with drool."

D stood up and brushed himself off. He realized he was clutching his bowie knife that was tucked into his belt. He prayed that it would never happen to him again.

He looked around and saw that he was back in Roger's house, the same way they left it.

"Sorry man," D said, "I could've killed you."

Roger saw that D was shaken but thankfully said in a cheerful tone, "Nah, get in line mate, there's a whole mess of people that want me dead... mainly for money."

D was not listening; he was trying to clear his mind from what happened and the thought of almost slitting Roger's throat.

The Irish reel stopped playing when Roger stopped the record player and hollered, "Let's get a move on!!! We're burning daylight!!"

Closing his eyes and then covering his ears, trying his hardest not to reconsider 'that' thought, D looked at him and said very irritatedly: "I'm right here, you old cranky geezer!!"

It's true, Roger was only three feet away from D, and the only thing separating them was the couch.

"Sorry, I was trying out how you Texans say it back home. Did I get it right?" he asked.

D answered, "If we were herding cattle, you'd be hired."

He got up and walked to Roger's spare bathroom. Once there, he looked in the mirror and clearly saw that he was in no condition yet to even step outside and go to work, so he splashed some water on his face and smelled his armpits. He wrinkled his nose as he went to reach for the soap and rinse his pits with warm water and the lather. He sniffed again and nodded a hint of 'that'll do.' When he turned to walk out, he saw Roger staring at him.

"That's disgusting!" Roger said.

"Who asked you?" D replied in his usual asshole manner.

He went back to the living room and kicked aside some metallic rubble that was in his way before reaching for his duffel bag and grabbing a pair of dark khaki cargo pants and a black Motorhead shirt.

"Hurry it up now mate, we'll be late," Roger said. It was surprising to see how one man last night could go through a whole bottle of Johnnie Walker and a crappy bottle of wine and still manage to be up to return to work.

D, however, was still shrugging it off, headache still intact but ignoring it. He walked into the bathroom, closed the door for fear of Roger absent-mindedly walking in and proceeded to put his new pair of pants on.

He wasn't wrong. No less than a minute later a knock came, and Roger barged in

with a glass of tea.

"There you are. Thought this could cheer you up a bi..." he stopped on that last word as he was staring at D's reflection in the mirror.

There were big slash marks on his chest, like an animal had a go at him. There were also scars and bruise marks all around his torso and back. If he had been a teenager, Roger would have notified the authorities about a domestic abuse case.

"DO YOU KNOCK GOD DAMMIT?!!" D roared as he took the tea and slammed the door in his face.

Roger stood there and pondered for a minute, like seeing

the door slammed in his face was not enough.

Who was this man from Texas? He remembered asking him about where he was from and where his parents were, but didn't get much out of him. He was starting to think that D might be some sort of hitman or hired government official sent in to 'clean' up a situation.

The door opened and D walked out. Roger stood there and waited for D to let loose on him, despite the fact that D was a guest in his home.

He was dumbfounded when he heard, "Sorry Rog, next time I need to just lock the door, but thanks for the tea." He handed the empty glass back to Roger and said, "Alright, let's roll!" as he walked out the door with the dogs right behind him.

Roger contemplated calling the police and telling them that there might be a dangerous man with him, but then they would just ask what he was doing there in the first place without a passport.

So many questions and so much stress, he decided against it and thought, 'Let's just wing it and see what happens.'

"You coming, Rog?" D yelled, and Roger hurried out of the house towards the jeep that both of them would have to get started over and over again.

CHAPTER 8
SMITHSTON URANIUM MINE

All seemed the same back at the Smithston Mine. Nobody paid any notice to the fact that one of their own had just died a very painful, brutal death.

Then again, 'accidents' did happen, and when you're a miner, it did come with the job.

With the jeep parked, D and Roger got out and went straight to Murray's office.

D was not looking forward to it. The fat manager almost seemed like he was waiting for a reason to accuse D of what happened yesterday. He also wondered what Murray had told the police yesterday. What crossed his mind even more was *what* D might be dealing with. Out of all the missions of doing services for the US Government, and especially Overstreet, this matter concerned him the most. The worker who died literally had his head crushed in by someone very powerful. D wondered too just who in their right frame of mind would be capable of that... but also if the culprit was even human.

He didn't even hear Roger's voice once they got to Murray's office.

D looked up as Roger continued, "Mate, you alright? I've been tryin' to get your attention."

D shook his head to clear his mind, "Yea, I'm good Rog, just dozed off for a bit, sorry," he said.

Roger knocked on the door, and in no less than three seconds it erupted open, and an even angrier Murray greeted them in the usual fashion that Roger seemed familiar with but one that D despised very much.

"YOU'RE BLOODY LATE, GODDAMMIT!! I SWEAR DO ANY OF YOU AMERICANS TAKE ANY BIT OF YOUR JOBS SERIOUSLY AT ALL?! IT'S A BLOODY OUTRAGE IT IS!!" screamed Murray.

Roger just gave a stupid smile like nothing was wrong, while D simply replied, "I'm sure it is. Now, are you finished?" He didn't even mean it in a polite fashion, it was more of a 'get out of my face or eat flaming death manner.'

"NO! I'M NOT BLOODY DONE, YOU USELESS SOD!!" roared Murray.

"Too Fuckin' Bad!" said D sternly.

Roger looked very awkward, as if he was in the middle of David Vs Goliath.

Murray was ready with another retort, but stopped once he heard those words come out of D's mouth. No matter how many times he tried, he could not break the American.

Murray, for the longest time, had been so used to getting things his way. From kissing corporate butt to sleeping around behind his wife's back, in his pudgy little mind he established himself in the hierarchy of the business world as manager of the mine. He could have any worker fired if he wanted. He could even take a day off from all the 'stress' that he endured without losing pay; which meant yelling for no reason other than to hear his stupid voice.

But he could not get D to succumb to his authority or ego. D was who he was, still standing as strong as ever against an incompetent moron.

"Now, where's the fuckin' cart? Or do we need to measure the size of our dicks first before we actually see keys in my fuckin' hand?!" D replied.

Murray closed his mouth, grabbed his keys from his pocket and threw them at D's chest.

Roger was about ready to hit the deck until D smirked and said, "That's one." He picked up the keys and walked out with

Roger, who was wiping sweat from his forehead.

As they walked down the stairs, Roger exclaimed, "I'm gonna give myself a heart attack one day with all this stress I'm goin' through. Couldn't you at least be a little more professional when it comes to people in high-ranking positions?"

D looked at him and Roger was afraid he might kill him right there and go on about his business in the mine. He only shook his head and walked off. Funny, but Roger seemed more hurt from that than being murdered by the gruff Texan.

As they followed the same path as they did yesterday, D was more quiet than usual. Probably still fuming about how Murray presented himself, yet Roger was very hesitant to ask what was wrong.

Not wanting the tension to be as thick as a Koala, he finally broke the silence. "So.... quite a nice six-pack you got on yourself, mate," Roger said.

D looked at him with a cocked-up eyebrow. This time he was the one who looked hesitant and awkward.

"Uhm, I mean... well, that is... what I meant to say was... Oh Fuck! You bloody say somethin' then," Roger said. D only looked away again.

Roger kept driving down into the tunnel of the mine when D finally spoke.

"How is that lard sack still alive?" he said.

Roger turned his head slightly to D and replied, "Oh come on now mate, he may be a git, but he's really not so bad once you get to know him. You, mate, just need to give people a chance. You're always so uptight about others that you make it a big deal when they're not as laid back as you are."

D rolled his eyes. "Oh, and giving a fat turd a chance at being an oversize, egotistical, drool-slobbering asshole?" D asked sarcastically. He continued, "Roger, sweet Jesus man, I don't even know you all that well, but if I didn't know any better, I'd say you're afraid of confrontations," D said.

Roger slammed on the brakes and turned to D.

"Now you listen to me mate, I may be old, crazy and a bit of a drunk, but I'm not afraid to show anyone I mean business. In fact, I told my dogs the other day that I didn't appreciate them shitting all over my inventions and that if it happened again, they were getting a time out!" Roger said proudly.

D retorted sarcastically, "Way to put your pooches in line. Give 'em a fucking time out! Again, I don't know you Roger, so I'm probably out of line for saying this, but grow a pair and stop letting people take advantage of who you are!"

Roger stared forward, staying quiet, and D got frustrated.

"Forget it. I think I'm just wasting my time talking sense to you. Just drive!" he said.

Roger still didn't say anything. What could he say? It was true he didn't know how to defend himself, but that's why he always used silence as a self-defense mechanism. It was the only thing he was ever good at while growing up, being raised by a single mother since age seven with one brother, an older one. Kids used to ridicule and humiliate him, but he always kept his composure in silence and allowed the insults to come. True, sticks and stones, but there was still a part deep inside Roger that made him want to fight back, but he couldn't. Once he came to his senses, he noticed D had already left without him. "Darrell? Ford? D?" he said and rushed after him in the darkness of the mine.

The smell was horrible; it was like being in the Middle East again. A memory he hoped he could put behind him. This one though was much stronger, and he remembered it all too well. His unit was investigating an old Nephite in Afghanistan where a missile from US forces had struck. He remembered walking inside and seeing dead bodies all around. It was usual to see men, possibly women, but children... that was a sight that still haunted him to this day. Some were infants....

CHAPTER 9

The smell inside the mine was all too familiar, the red slime remained where it was too. D walked quietly into the tunnel, flashlight and Smith and Wesson intact. The air and atmosphere was deathly silent, and he could almost imagine something popping out of nowhere from the darkness and brutally tearing him to shreds. On the other hand, he was used to it. The scars that Roger saw earlier this morning were a grim reminder of D's past.

"D... where you at, mate?" Roger called from afar, but D didn't answer back.

No less than five seconds later, D heard scuffling in the distance. Not from Roger, but from the sides and front. Impossible.

The tunnel has only two ways to go: front and back, so why would he hear it on the sides?

He stopped, kneeled and listened very carefully. It was quiet. D couldn't hear Roger calling for him anymore. He probably got lost.

'Moron,' D thought.

He stared into the darkness with his light, but even that wasn't as powerful as what he was expecting it to be. He should have brought his own, at least it would be able to shine for a couple hundred yards. It wasn't enough though. He could not see at all.

The scuffling started again in the same areas; he stayed perfectly still to get a trace of the origin.

It was happening in a pattern, a pattern that he had heard

before. From front, left, right to front, right, left, he briefly glanced to his sides from a peripheral perspective but could not make out what was doing it.

The last time this happened was ten years ago, in New Mexico. Somewhere in Cimarron, where he had to investigate possible terrorist activities in the mountains... it stopped.

His heart was pounding, not out of fear, but adrenaline. Whatever was making those sounds was not going to live very much longer.

D could get very trigger-happy when on edge.

A new noise started to develop, a voice.

It was much lower and much more terrifying. It was like listening to a huge animal that was hungry but patiently stalking its prey until it had an opening. Only this animal could possibly be fifty feet tall... in a tunnel about ten feet tall and eight feet in diameter.

At this point, D was not sure if his pistol would be any help at all.

Nevertheless, if he goes down, he would take whatever it was with him.

"What the fuck are you?" D whispered.

He then heard thumping, slow thumping but heavy, heading straight for him. He stood his ground and prepared himself for what approached, his heart racing with excitement and wondered, 'What the hell is that?'

Out in the distance of the tunnel, he saw a silhouette in a clear but misty form start to manifest. He held his breath as it started to take shape. The eyes formed and were glowing... red. The form was that of a little girl, no less than eight years of age. She didn't say anything, but she just stared with those piercing red eyes.

D got up and stood there too, staring at the girl.

She was of middle eastern descent, with clothes that were tattered and torn. He had seen her before, only not alive.

"Kid, you alright?" D asked, holstering his pistol.

She just stood there and watched him. This wasn't a curious look most kids gave when they met strangers, this look was pure evil. This girl wanted blood.

"Are you alright?" he asked again. "How did you get in here? Are your parents around?"

The girl extended her right hand slowly and gave a flick of her fingers. D felt a sharp pain in his heart.

He'd been used to pain, but this one was like no other. He was on the ground, writhing and growling in pain. It was like someone was using a dull butter knife and twisting it around in his chest. He was lying on his back when he looked up and saw her standing over him.

"What... are... you?" he gritted through his teeth.

She looked at him and opened her mouth to speak. D saw the razor-sharp teeth emerging from her gums. She said in a raspy, growling voice, "Found you!" Then aimed for his throat to bite.

Fortunately, D could work through pain.

He grabbed at her throat and held her at bay. She was the one writhing now, her hands clawing and legs kicking at him.

D got to his feet slowly, the pain in his chest still throbbing, while holding her out in front of him.

He reeled back his arm with all his might and threw her forward. She landed on both of her feet and hands and started to crawl in a spider-like movement.

D's eyes widened in horror and surprise; he then grabbed his pistol and fired. She was obviously too fast for the bullets.

Not wanting to waste any more ammo, he pulled out his bowie knife.

She pounced once again at D's throat, and D plunged his knife into her chest. He lifted her up to prevent any accidental bites. She hissed at D and then fell silent. He dropped her once she stopped struggling, and she fell to the ground as lifeless as a rag doll.

She didn't move.

The pain was slowing in D's chest, but he still dropped to his knees to collect himself. As he breathed slow and steady, he looked at the girl's body to make sure she was dead. He crawled over to see if she was still breathing, though he highly doubted it. No one could survive with that much force into a big knife like D's.

He put his two fingers to her neck to check her pulse.

Nothing. She was gone.

D took a big breath and closed his eyes; he then muttered a small little prayer, "Father, forgive me."

That was when two hands clasped around him, and he saw that the girl was still alive. She then threw herself on him to where her hands were still on his neck, but she was standing on top of his chest. He wasn't surprised that he was losing breath. She wasn't human.

She stared into his eyes with the crimson ones that were her own and said, "GOD'S NOT HERE!!"

At that, her form started to deteriorate and morph into what he would think was an overgrown pit bull with very sharp teeth, hind paws, but with human hands... gnarled, terrifying-looking human hands.

The pressure from the creature was slowly taking a lot out of D, but he reached back for his bowie knife. He stabbed the creature in the head repeatedly, blood spewing all over the place and onto D. It toppled over, and D slit its throat for good measure before kicking it near the wall of the mine.

He watched as the creature went into its death spasms until it moved no more. That's when it started to dissolve into what D noticed, the red slime that covered the walls. Once the body was gone, everything went quiet again.

D's chest felt heavy and bruised, he even thought he felt something snap, but that could have been a joint popping. He felt his throat, and sure enough he was bleeding. The claws had dug at him pretty bad.

He turned to walk back out and noticed he was never

alone to begin with. Roger stood there, pale as a ghost and sweating profusely from his forehead. He had witnessed the whole ordeal, girl, creature and all.

The only words Roger could muster were, "What in the flyin' fuckadilly was that?!!"

CHAPTER 10

Once outside, Roger couldn't hold back any longer and kept pounding questions at D.

"What did you see, mate? Who was that girl? Why were her bloody eyes red? Oh yea, did she have a dog? Was that why you were attacked?" Roger kept asking.

D was tired, annoyed and angry. Roger knew what happened but kept asking questions to which he already knew the answers. Somehow D couldn't blame him. What could Roger do? What could he have done? This was a first for him as well. He wasn't a soldier like D. Just an ordinary man with too much time on his hands to make dumb inventions.

D took slow, steady breaths and closed his eyes. That was always his way of calming down and bringing himself back to the present, despite the pain.

The cart came to a stop and D opened his eyes to see that they were back at Murray's Office building.

"Damn, that was fast," D said.

Roger got out of the cart and asked, "What do we tell him? I mean, he does need to know what happened. It's the only way he can make a decision to close the mine indefinitely until further notice."

D stopped him. "Calm down!" he said sternly, more like an order. "Before we do anything, you need to tell me what you saw," D said.

Roger looked at him as though he had asked him to cut his own balls off. "I... I... well, the girl... and the dog..." he fumbled his words.

D had to intervene. "Roger, you know what you saw, and I'm a prime example of it." He displayed himself covered in that creature's blood and his own. "But I need to hear from you right now that you're gonna stand by what you saw. Stand up to him and tell him what you saw."

D knew already from what he'd seen from Roger that this might not work. He had to suck it up though. If he remained silent, it wouldn't just make D look bad, but more workers would get killed.

"I... OK," Roger said half-heartedly.

"Alright then, let's do this," D said.

He was a man on a mission, to prove to Murray that he does have a problem. It was getting Roger to snap out of it that was the difficult part.

The light was still on in his office, which meant he hadn't gone to lunch yet. Unless he was eating inside, which D highly doubted. For a man who cares little about his job and workers, why bother staying for lunch?

Roger knocked on the door, and both men heard in response, "I'm busy, do us a favor and piss off!"

Roger turned to walk away. D grabbed his shirt and pulled him back, smacking him over the head and pointing at the door again for Roger to knock.

He did so once more. "I said FUCK OFF! I'm having lunch! Can't a man eat in peace?!" roared Murray.

Roger looked to D for help but was answered once D kicked in the door.

It was a very disturbing sight to see.

Murray, in his large 'frame' called a body, was on his knees half naked with his shirt off and underwear still on. A woman who looked in her mid-forties was dressed like a school-teacher with high-heeled boots and a baton. She gave one look at Roger and then sneered. She then saw D and licked her lips. D was very uncomfortable, not the time or place.

Murray fumbled to his feet and swore under his breath while doing so.

"So, this is lunch?" D asked. "Whose?" he pressed on.

"Wanna find out?" the woman asked.

Despite still being in a bit of pain, D was tempted to find out afterwards. His concentration, however, came back once Murray slammed his fists on the desk.

"ARE YOU FUCKING MAD?!" he screamed. "YOU'VE NO RIGHT TO BARGE IN HERE UNANNOUNCED!!"

He looked D up and down and Roger, who was still sweating and blushing from the whole ordeal he just witnessed. "What happened to you blokes?" he said.

D moved in. "You've got a problem, Murray. We just got back from the mine and... sorry ma'am, you'll need to excuse us," he addressed the woman.

She walked out of the room but brushed D lightly on the arm, hinting interest. Funny, D felt something soothe through his arm once she did that. Probably just a blood rush.

He kept his cool though. Funny how she wasn't more interested in him being covered in blood.

"See ya around, Murray love, same time next week?" she asked, putting a wad of cash in her bosom.

Murray gave her an incredulous look and fumbled his words. "Uh... yes... same check up tomorrow, doctor, glad the infection is fine."

She looked confused and then said sarcastically, "Right! Infection." Then turned and walked away.

Murray then focused on the two gentlemen, and that term was used loosely. "This had better be bloody good you two. Now what is it?" Murray demanded.

Roger handed him a piece of clothing very nervously. "Uh, your shirt sir," he said.

Murray grabbed the shirt and shouted, "WHAT THE FUCK DO YOU WANT?!"

D continued, "We just got back from the mine. The red slime that's all over the tunnels? It's what's responsible for your men dying."

Murray looked confused. "Red slime? You mean to say the red slime is what crushed that man's head in? Come off it, Ford," he said.

D wasn't backing down. "NO! The slime is taking on a mind of its own. It can form into anything it wants to. In this case, for the worker yesterday, it took the form of Bigfoot or some other thing that's capable of doing something of the sort."

Murray snorted, "Preposterous!" he said. Either he didn't want to believe it or didn't care at all about the situation. "You had to bring up the damn Bigfoot issue again."

As usual, D lost his cool. "Listen to me Fucktard! I just got out of a battle with one of the many forms that it can take, and you're calling it preposterous? You've got a problem! Where is this red slime coming from?" D demanded.

Murray still wasn't having any of it. "Rubbish. There's obviously some sort of animal down there that's causing these problems and having a go at my workers. This is why you're here, to kill it or remove it. I'm assuming you've done just that based on your appearance."

The only thing keeping D from strangling him was the desk between them.

"It was NO DAMN ANIMAL!" D stated. "It took the form of a little girl and tried to kill me, then it took the form of another creature, in the form of a dog!"

Murray just looked at him, despite the fact that D was still trying to prove his point, it was still very awkward standing there trying to talk sense to a half-naked fat man.

He pondered for a moment before asking, "So you mean to tell me... that you had your arse handed to you by a little brat and her doggy? This is what the US Government has on its payroll?" referring to D.

Murray then turned his attention to Roger, who was rocking back and forth on his feet. "Well, what about you? Did you see it?" he demanded.

Roger looked at him, then to D, who gave him the look of 'Tell Him!' Roger shifted a little and Murray demanded again, "Mr. Blarnsworth, did you see what this man just saw? Is he telling the truth?"

Murray knew Roger pretty well. He knew Roger wouldn't lie. This was out of fear though.

"Uh, there was... just an animal, sir," Roger said nervously.

D was dumbfounded. He just stared at Roger with a hint of betrayal.

"An animal? That's all? What of this little girl?" Murray pressed on.

Roger replied again nervously, "There was... uh..."

"BLARNSWORTH!" roared Murray.

Roger yelped, "NO! No. There was no girl!"

Murray had a vein in his neck that was about to burst. D had stopped looking at Roger and now stared at the floor, anger on his face. 'The Dumbshit! Can't grow a pair if his life depended on it!' D thought.

Murray sat down at his chair, pinched the bridge of his nose for five seconds, then spoke. "I told that blasted Overstreet that allowing you to come here was a big mistake. That it was a waste of my valuable time to go out of my way and show you around. YOU! MR. FORD! are the most useless, lying ingrate I have ever met in my entire career! Even if there was a girl in the mine. To have her nail your arse to the cross is pretty pathetic for an American. Both of you get out of my office! Finish your investigation tomorrow, but after that I want you gone, Mr. Ford. You and your 'special set of skills' that Overstreet told me about. All of it. GONE!"

D couldn't say anything, and it pissed him off even more. If there was one thing he hated, it was being betrayed, plus embarrassment to go with it.

"And as for this 'little girl and dog' story, here's my response to that," Murray said, and spat on D's boot.

Blood, dismemberment and death filled D's head at what

that fat sack of shit just did to him, and all he could think of was doing just those things to him.

Instead, he replied, "That's two!" and walked out, Roger in tow but staying slightly further behind.

He could sense D's vibes; he knew he royally fucked up.

They walked down from Murray's office and straight for the jeep. Roger hopped in the driver's side but noticed that D walked past the passenger's side, not getting in the car.

"Uh... mate, the car's right here," he said.

D ignored him and kept walking. Though he was being ignored he continued on, "D! C'mon now mate, I know I screwed up in there. But can't you give a man a break?"

"Break this!" D said and gave him his middle finger without turning to face him.

Roger stood there and sunk his head. 'Way to go, Roger,' he thought. 'Can't even tell someone anything without your balls shriveling up.'

Roger turned the ignition and the engine sputtered; he rubbed his head then slammed the driver's wheel. He then buried his face into his arms and felt little stings in his eyes.

CHAPTER 11

D walked along the grounds of the mine complex and asked a worker where he could get a good signal for his phone. When pointed in the right direction, he made his way over there and made his call.

He dialed several numbers and spoke in short words like, "OO111673... US Special Forces... Direct Line Overstreet... Codename D."

A few moments later, a familiar voice rang out, "Ford, I was expecting you to call as soon as you flew in. What kept you?" Overstreet said.

"Same shit, different day, sir. I've looked into the main areas of attacks and have found evidence of numerous foreign life along the walls and grounds of the deceased," D said.

Overstreet chuckled and replied, "Ford, we're buddies, remember? Cut out the sweet talk and speak English, dammit!"

D took a breath and continued on, "Well, things have been very interesting here, I'll tell you what."

D looked around to make sure no one was around or listening, then went on.

"I've only had one body so far drop dead on me, literally. He was still alive, but not for long. I'm sure you know who Murray is?" D asked.

Overstreet groaned. "Oh yea! Cheeky fellow, isn't he?" Overstreet said in a poor Australian accent.

D ignored him. "Well, he certainly won't take other people's sayings into consideration. I've given him clear evidence of what has been going on, and he's still oblivious to the fact that there are problems arising," D said.

"What kind of evidence?" Overstreet asked. This time he had his superior's full attention and D explained all he had seen, from the worker with the crushed head to the demon girl/dog.

Overstreet was quiet for a moment and then asked, "Ford? Have you been drinking?" D was taken off guard, not him too!

"Captain, why would I lie about this? Haven't I always come clean with my assignments and duties?" D asked defensively.

Overstreet spoke up, "Settle down Ford. I ask only because I need to report to these other bureaucrats back in D.C. about your findings. I'm sorry, but what you're telling me, it all sounds ridiculous. I trust you; I really do, but you're talking madness. This is not why I sent you over there!"

D rolled his eyes. The one man he could count on to understand his situation and believe what he had seen was now calling him a liar.

"You sent me here to clean house and find out who was killing these people, but you never mentioned anything about monsters," D said.

"Monsters? What are you talking about? Forget it Ford, it seems you've already ruffled enough feathers. Finish up and come home. That's an Order!" Overstreet retaliated.

D pondered, then said, "You want proof? Fine! I'll give you proof!" and he hung up.

Before he could do anything else, D had to sit down and collect himself.

After all, it's amazing how he had been attacked earlier, and yet now the pain and exhaustion was catching up.

D had always been like that though, working through pain. It was only weakness leaving the body. Years of training with the military and with different martial artists who basically inflicted more pain on him than his marine background, kept him going and was a reassurance that he could take anything thrown at him and keep moving forward.

He remembered a time when the enemy during the Iraq war had snuck up behind him and buried a dagger into D's right side. As much as it hurt, D was not concentrating on that. Instead, once the feelings of surprise had left him, he reached backwards with his left arm and held the enemy's head while taking the thumb of his right hand and jabbing it deep into the man's eyeball, scooping it out. D was more interested in killing the man than he was about his wound.

When taken back for medical attention, officers said he wouldn't make it and that the wound was too deep. The next day, however, they were surprised to see D sitting up in his military cot eating sour patch. Nobody understood it, even D knew that he shouldn't be alive. Some higher order must have been watching over him that day. That was something D would never understand, but it was what encouraged him to seek better training and help him to cope with pain and injuries while still getting the upper hand in combat.

He came back to his senses when he realized he was dozing off. He opened his eyes and thought about the two people who didn't believe him and how another was too much of a coward to speak up, as well as the fact that more workers would die.

He needed to center himself, he was under too much stress right now, and he had to concentrate to bring him back to reality. He closed his eyes and concentrated on his 'island paradise' again. This time no distractions.

He returned to where he was this morning, relaxing again and finding solace in the waves that crashed. As he lay on the sand, he felt another shadow hover over him. He thought it might be that woman again. He opened his eyes, and sure enough... was wrong again. He would've wished to hear Roger's voice instead of what he saw next. There standing over him was a man, but this man looked like he had been through hell. His face only had one eye and the other an empty socket, with parts of his skull missing. The flesh where his lips should have been was ripped off, and all of his skeletal jaw was visible. His clothing too was shredded and torn, with deep gashes and wounds showing. The man was holding a long, slimy substance in his left hand, and when D took notice, he saw that he was holding his own intestines. D rolled out of the way and into his defensive position. But this is his sanctuary, his peace. Why was it being disturbed so much? It's never happened to him before. D didn't say anything though as the zombified figure just stared at him with that one eye and jaw hanging down. For a minute D thought that this figure looked familiar, like something he had seen before... or caused. He waited to see what would be the next thing that would happen. D's muscles were getting tense in the dream due to the adrenaline rush, but still maintained his position. If it tried anything D would rip its head off, or what was left of it. The zombie spoke, the same words D heard before... "Found you!" D's eyes widened as the walking cadaver launched itself at him.

CHAPTER 12

D awoke and was breathing hard, 'what in the hell is wrong with me?' he thought.

He started to look around to see his surroundings and saw that he was still in the same place as before, where the worker had shown him the area of good reception. The only difference was that it was now 4:15pm on his phone clock. He had been asleep for about three to four hours. The dream, though, felt like it was only about twenty minutes or more.

He heard people shouting and calling out to one another. He got up to his feet and saw that everyone was rushing towards the mine... THE mine.

D already knew something bad had happened and rushed down there too, hoping it was not too late.

The mine was pitch black, aside from the lights from all the workers that were also occupying inside, it was still dark. Everyone was yelling, questioning one another as to what had happened or, as D heard, "Who's snuffed it this time?"

He pushed his way forward until he saw a huddle of men surrounding something. He ordered, "Move!" and they dispersed automatically. He could hear the gossiping all around him, asking questions like, "Who's he?" or "Is that the American?"

When the huddle disbanded, D took one look, and his eyes widened again.

The same cadaver that he saw in his dream was lying before him, same eye socket and all.

D walked forward and knelt near the body. A fresh kill. The one in the dream was already a bit deteriorated.

The crowd drew near and D said, "I need everyone to clear the area now. Call the supervisor and have him meet me down here on the double!"

The workers looked at each other as if they were wondering if they should do something or not.

He shouted, "MOVE!" and at once they departed for the entrance, taking care not to touch the walls.

It was now pitch black again, and all the workers cleared.

At least D knew where he left his flashlight.

Pulling out his pistol, he shined and aimed all around to make sure he was entirely clear.

Whatever did this was still around, and D was not going to take any chances again.

But why did he see the dead body in his dream before it happened, or had it happened while he was sleeping? The question that still stayed on D's mind was why did this cadaver look so familiar? ...

As he stared at the body, his mind started to wander, and he slowly lowered his weapon and light as he drifted into his past, and D now realized where he had seen it before.

Afghanistan 2006

D and his unit were wandering the old Nephite building again. A man suddenly ambushes D from behind and plunges his dagger into D's right side. D yells in surprise and pain as he feels the blade slit through flesh and muscle. Anger fills his head and D grabs the man's head with his left hand and pulls him in, then takes his right hand and thumb and jabs it into the man's left eye and plucks it out. The man tears away and howls in pain as he falls onto the floor, blood spurting from his empty socket. Despite the pain and fear of blacking out, anger and adrenaline take control of D's body, and he starts pummeling the man. The only thing he sees before anything else is red in his eyes. After he comes to his senses, he sees his handiwork on what he did to his enemy. It's a mess. He wonders what came over him before he falls to the ground too, after losing so much blood.

Looking down, he realized now that this body was the man from Afghanistan. Everything down to a 'T.'

None of this made any sense, which is probably also the reason why no one believed him.

He thought to himself for a moment and started to consider his own sanity. "I'm losing my mind," he said to himself.

He shined his light and weapon in both directions again to see if anything might show up. He just remembered he was injured from his last venture inside this mine. The blood had dried now, but he could now feel his body starting to ache. The adrenaline was wearing off, and he wasn't sure if he would be up for another round. This time, if it did attack, it might kill him.

He kneeled again near the corpse, the smell still lingering in the tunnels. He turned his head and light back and forth, checking to see if anything might be around. Nothing.

He heard a scuffle behind him, and he was quick to aim his firearm in that direction. "Please don't shoot... I'm sorry!" cried a man in overalls and headgear. A worker.

D lowered his weapon, breathing through his teeth before asking, "Didn't I say all workers out? Leave. Now!"

The worker hesitated, then said, "Please, that man, he was a friend of mine. Let me take his wallet. Give it to his family," he said.

D observed the man, he was Pakistani. 'Migrant worker probably, poor bastard getting stuck in this dump,' D thought. But he stood his ground.

"NO! Get Out!" he said.

The worker pressed, "Please sir?" he begged.

D contemplated shooting near the ground where he stood to get him out, but before he could he witnessed two dark forms rise up and grab the man and start pulling him into the red slime.

D rushed forward to grab his extending hand to try and pull him out. He saw though that it was in vain.

The man started to scream in agony as D witnessed his flesh start to become one with the slime. He could see, however, that the tissue, bone, vessels and organs of the worker started to melt.

D still hung on until he just closed his eyes and let go, the remains of the worker got sucked in.

D swore under his breath until he heard an inhuman growl erupt from all around him. It was like hearing a man's moan combined with a predator's call. He quickly sobered up and looked around. Waiting for what came next. That's when he noticed the other body was gone.

Now D felt the hairs on his neck stand on end. He had the feeling that something was watching him from all sides. He stood still, limited his breathing to a few deep ones, and closed his eyes. Once again, he was trying to find the source of the sound.

The moaning started again, that inhuman call of terror.

D tried to get a fix on it, paying very close attention, not just to sound but feel as well.

D opened his eyes and stared forward; the moaning now was fixated right behind him.

He raised his pistol up to his head, hoping that whatever was behind him would see it and run off.

Instead, he felt like he was being stalked. This thing was not afraid.

Slowly but calmly, D turned around, his heart racing for what new evil he might see.

When he turned the full 180 degrees, he saw it.

Standing just the same as it had in the dream, the dead cadaver stood perfectly still. The empty, yet still bleeding, eye socket being the closest to D.

He stood his ground though and sized him up. He may not have seen a zombie, monster or ghost before, but that wouldn't stop him.

Pistol still raised near his head, he aimed, waiting for the attack, but none came. D heard something else, the sound of pitter patter. Like a dog running towards its master... DOG?!!

D spun around and watched as the same pit bull-like monster raced towards him from the darkness.

It pounced, ready to take D down with one chomp, but he anticipated this move very quickly. On instinct, D bent backwards and dropped to his back, the demon dog barely missing him by inches. It tumbled and hit the dead worker head-on in the knees, collapsing him on top of it.

D quickly jumped up and looked toward the ground. He dropped his pistol and couldn't find it.

He heard an ear-splitting scream and turned to see that the zombie was coming straight at him with arms flailing all over the place.

D pulled out his Bowie knife and prepared for impact. As the dead worker closed in, D ducked under the flying arms and sliced in one motion the zombie's rib cage.

Of course, it wouldn't feel anything, it was already dead. It turned around and tried another attack, but met with the same result. This time though, as D turned to the walking cadaver, with careful and quick aim he threw his blade at the back of the worker's head. It stopped instantly!

D waited, it was only a matter of time until the left-over brain cells gave out, and it would fall.

The zombie turned around, and D saw how deep the knife went, he could see the tip of the blade pointing out of its forehead. It screamed one last inhuman call just before it fell face-first into the ground.

D paused for a bit more just in case it should move again. After a minute, he moved forward to retrieve his knife.

With one swift jerk, the blade came out. D wiped the blood on his pants and sheathed it. He picked up his flashlight and shined with what little he could to see all around. There was still the dog. Where was it?

He looked around but saw no form or being around him. Walking forward slowly, he wasn't sure exactly which way was out or in for the tunnel.

He kicked something hard, and as he looked down, he saw the barrel of his Smith and Wesson lying on the ground.

Still looking straight, he bent down slowly to retrieve his weapon, but as soon as he grabbed it, the jaws of the demon dog appeared from nowhere and clamped down on his arm.

Fangs sinking deep into his flesh, he roared in pain as he struggled with the canine, falling to the ground but taking care not to touch the slime. The dog was jerking its head violently, and D was afraid it might pull his arm clean out of its socket. He'd been bitten by dogs before, but none compared to this. It was like having a vise with jagged edges pressing down continuously.

He reached back for his knife, but the pain was unbearable. He could hear the dog growling still as it started to pull D into the red slime. D tried to pull back with all his strength but could see it was useless. The dog was much stronger since he was not of this earth, and D was getting weak. The last fight took a lot out of him, and it was enough to do him in at the moment.

D waited as the hellish mutt pulled him closer in, and D closed his eyes, ready to feel the molten hand of death that consumed the other worker.

RATTATTATTATTA!!!

He heard this as he saw the dog let go of its grip on D and bound backwards with the barrage of bullets that struck it. It spasmed and clawed at the air as the bullets came flying at it until it lay on the ground, lifeless and in a pool of blood.

D lay face down on the ground, his good arm to his side while the other barely inches away from the slime and dog, bloodied and mangled.

He glanced in the direction the bullets came from and saw a shape approaching. He could hear the voice speaking in and

out vaguely. "D... don't die mate... D... No!" He heard a familiar Australian voice. The last thing he remembered before he
blacked out.

*He was fishing. Lying back in his boat he patiently waited to feel the
bite that would signal 'DINNER' time. He gazed around and saw a
clear blue ocean surrounding him while the summer breeze brushed
his face. 'This is how life should be,' he thought to himself. 'No wor-
ries, No Fear, No PROBLEMS!!!' They were the three goals he lived
by, and it's worked out so far for him. "Find me," he heard a voice
whisper. He cocked his head to the side to see if it would happen
again. Nothing. He continued fishing again until he heard it again.
This time it was different. "Save us,"....*

CHAPTER 13

He opened his eyes.

He saw medical equipment and pictures of stupid plants and animals covering the walls.

A hospital. D hated hospitals. People died in hospitals.

He looked at the TV in the corner to his right and saw some show that usually airs in Australia. He then glanced in the other corner, and there was Roger sound asleep on the couch nearby. He looked miserable, like he had just watched one of his dogs die... dog... DOG!!!

He was sitting up quickly and regretted it instantly.

His right arm was bandaged and set in a splint. He couldn't even feel his fingertips.

That thing must have torn it up so badly that the nerves were not functioning as they should. At least he still had the arm.

"Crikey mate, you scared the shit outta me!" Roger said, startled. He got up to calm D down and lowered him back to the bed. "That was one nasty bite you got there. Thought for sure you were a goner. Thank Odin you're still in one piece though," Roger continued.

D inhaled and exhaled in a steady beat as he stared at the ceiling. He then asked, "How long was I out?"

Roger replied, "A day or so. Thought you were gonna shoot out for more, though."

D looked at him, and Roger raised his hands in surrender. "Sorry mate, the nurses and I were all taking bets on when you would wake up," he said and pointed to the door.

D looked to see a group of hospital workers and nurses chuckling and giggling. "I won," he said matter of factly.

The head nurse walked to him and paid him fifty Australian dollars. The man looked at D and said, "G'day mate," and walked out, ushering the others to get back to work.

D looked at Roger again. "I'm only worth fifty bucks? Should that be a good thing here in Australia?"

Roger laughed. "Naw, just a good laugh, that's all, but at least I got something in return!" he said, showing D the money.

"Lucky you," D said. "By the way, what does a pig say when you add a 'Y' at the beginning?" he asked.

Roger just stared at him and replied, "Huh?"

With a quick but painful reflex action, D snatched the money out of Roger's hand and said, "YOINK!"

Roger barely had time to react, but when he did, he was appalled. "Oi, that's mine!" he declared.

"This is blood money, and goes to the one who lost blood, and I do believe that's me!" D stated.

Roger stood his ground. "Like Bloody Hell it does." He stepped forward.

D replied, "Roger, arm or no arm, I will beat you mercilessly!"

He stopped. He knew that D was a special type of man and didn't want to push it. He grunted and sat back down. D pondered for a moment, trying to determine the next course of action for himself.

He could easily just get up and walk out of the hospital. If he did leave, he would just let his arm set and heal on its own while continuing his investigation. He wanted to leave; he HATED hospitals. Plus, if questions arose from the hospital staff as to where he went, he knew the good ol' US of A government would handle it.

Just like all the other 'accidents.'

He started to get up, but Roger pushed him gently back down.

"Not so fast, mate. You can't fool me with your body language." D was being stubborn.

"I know you want to leave, but that's not going to happen," Roger said sternly.

D still pushed forward. "I need to get on the phone and make a call. Let me up!" he insisted.

Roger gripped his shoulders to calm him and said, "D, your phone was destroyed. I'm sorry, but it smashed when that dog was fighting with you."

D stared at him for a few seconds and asked, "You were there?"

Roger shrunk a little and said, "Yea... I was... after you and I separated, I wanted to tell you that I would go back and tell Murray the truth this time. Only I heard you on the phone and heard you say something about 'proof.' I knew what you meant, and well..."

He reached into his pack and pulled out a familiar object that D had seen a while back.

The bracelet that could put a hole in a barn door.

D stared at it and came to the realization.

"You killed it?" he asked.

"I think so," Roger replied. He sat back down on the couch and continued, "I didn't think. I just saw you getting butchered and hauled into that red crap and just shot at it."

He was looking down; D knew this man had probably never killed anything in his life. Probably not even a bug.

D started to relax and took his steady breaths again; the pain was still throbbing. He was trained to ignore pain and move forward, but he was human, and sometimes it still crept up on him.

"I've never killed anythin' before, not even a bug," Roger continued, and D raised his eyes at the mention of bug.

He looked at D and asked calmly, "Is this the same as what you've done before? You know, taking a life?"

D raised himself up a bit. "Try humans next time. It hurts

a hell of a lot more."

Roger gave him an incredulous look and said, "Christ, mate! I'm trying to open up a bit, and you just toss in the wallop, sauce and all. You're not still mad at me, are you?"

D slunk into his bed, not in shame but pain. "I don't sugar coat shit, Rog; I say it like it is. After so many years of doing what I do best and getting the job done, you learn to just adjust to it and live with it."

Roger looked down again. The words he wanted to hear were not going to be said. Comfort was what he was looking for, but from his new companion he would get none.

"Never mind, forget I said anything," Roger dejectedly said.

"Don't take it so hard. When you react to a situation where someone's life is in jeopardy, you don't think, you act. If you think too long, then that life is already gone. Yes, it's true, acting quickly could also land you in a heap of trouble, but we have to take that risk in order to help someone. In the end, if it means that you were trying to save a life, then you've done well," D said honestly.

Roger looked up at him. So this new friend did have feelings after all, but he masked it very well.

"In time you'll get over it, but don't feed the fire," he continued.

"What do you mean 'feed the fire'?" Roger asked.

D glanced in his direction and explained, "Guilt, fear, and shame! They're fire. Don't feed them because it'll eat you alive and keep doing so until you are only a shell of your former self. The vibes that come from you latch onto others and make them feel your pain and sorrow, whether they want to or not. In the end, the people who are close to you and love you with all of their heart will slowly start to walk away because you allowed that fire to grow."

Roger thought for a moment, then asked, "You've killed before and were not talkin' 'bout animals either. You're a soldier, and I know what soldiers have done in war. Is it any different? Taking a human life? What would that make you?"

D stared hard into Roger's face, who gulped a little at what he had just asked of him.

Roger recalled in his head a man he knew who visited the United States and started making fun of a bloke from Texas himself. The man returned with a little tip for Roger. "Any little thing you say and it's 'Them's Fightin' Words!'" He would hate himself later, for now he waited for a reply.

"Depends on who's the animal," D said.

Roger understood what he meant. Humans were an unusual species, but even then, their actions could justify who's pure and who's scum in society.

A knock came from the door, and both men turned to face a man who, by his age, was ranging in his fifties with a tan trench coat and red tie. He had no facial hair, but even if he had, it wouldn't hide the lines and creases of stress and anxiety that came with his job. He looked like a cross between Colin Hay of Men at Work and actor Paul Hogan.

D automatically recognized him as the detective Murray was speaking with during his first investigation at the mine.

The man introduced himself, "G'Day gentlemen," he said in a stern but tired voice. "My name is Sergeant Johnathan O'Hara with the Australian Federal Police. I'm here to speak with our young American friend here," he continued as if reading off a note card. "Two days being here already suffering a substantial amount of damage to himself. Not a very good way to enjoy our beautiful country now, is it, Mr....?"

Roger spoke before D could. "G'Day Jon, what's the good word? Haven't seen you in the last... oh... two weeks? You know, the crocodile incident?"

Sergeant O'Hara gave him a look and pressed on. "As I was saying, Mr....?"

D extended his good hand. "Ford, Darrell Ford." He shook his hand. "US Special Forces."

O'Hara continued. "Ah yes, that's what Murray was saying, that you're part of a special task force from America here to… as he claims… 'Muck about his mine and spread… pardon the language… red shit all over his place,'" O'Hara said.

D just cocked his right eye; Murray was lying, and D started to assume that this detective might be led on to believe something that was false accusations.

Roger stepped in. "That's a lie! That red shit was already there!"

O'Hara turned to look at him. "How would you know? Were you with them?" he asked.

"Well, of course I was with them. I saw everything with my own eyes! The red stuff was already there. It's been there since the plant accident. We were thinking that it was just part of what happened. But then the red stuff started to kill people, and that's why D… Mr. Ford, here, was trying to investigate everything that was happening with courtesy through the US. He tried to save the workers."

O'Hara turned to D and asked, "How about you, mate? What's your story?"

D looked at Roger, who was looking back at D, reassuring him that he wouldn't back down ever again.

"You heard the man, Sergeant, clear as day," D said.

O'Hara continued, "Murray claims that the mine was functioning as normal as possible and that all of the accidents and such have started happening as soon as involvement from your country began."

D said nothing. Murray might be paying him off to stick to his story and not D's. It was clear that Murray did not like Americans or, for that matter, D.

O'Hara leaned in. "Tell me, Mr. Ford, is it true that your involvement in this matter has caused these tragedies?" O'Hara asked.

"Are you asking for a fact or an opinion, detective? Your question almost sounds misleading," D replied. O'Hara pressed further, "Well, I am curious, Mr. Ford; I want to know more about what it is that you and the American government are up to here in Australia. There have been many inquiries as to what the presence of the United States around the Uranium mine is doing there. Now I know you know what I am talking about, Mr. Ford, and I want to know now what you and your country had to do with Mr. Dunkler's mine."

D started to lift himself from off the bed. Roger made a move to stop him but backed off once D gave him 'the look'. He moved his legs to the floor and was squaring up now to the Detective, who didn't seem to flinch either.

"You don't like me very much, detective, but it's cool. I'm not a very likable person. I cannot vouch for what my government is doing in your country, but I can tell you right now that I neither know nor care. What they choose to do is their own business, and mine is my own. I had nothing to do with what had happened in those mines. If you still have reservations about my answers, go find some fuckin' proof. These are the rantings of an obese shithead who hates everyone and his mother. I'm not going to tell you how to do your job, but back off of mine... Detective!" D ordered.

By now both the detective and the mercenary were squaring up, neither of them backing down.

A crash broke the tension as O'Hara, in a split second, raised his pistol towards the sound. The detective had his hand on his holster the moment D talked back to him. This man was clearly on edge about something.

"Oh, fuck me!" cried Roger, who had accidentally pushed a lamp over the table near the doorway. "Bloody Hell man, what's with you?!!" Roger exclaimed at the sight of O'Hara's pistol.

The sergeant looked at his weapon and immediately came to his senses. He holstered his pistol and turned back to D. "Terribly sorry about that. We will continue this later, Mr. Ford." He turned to leave without saying anything to Roger.

The nurses came in to see what had crashed to the floor and saw both men staring at the doorway where the detective had disappeared to. "Everything alright? We heard a crash," one of the nurses said.

D sat on the bed while Roger made up a little white lie as to what happened in the room. When the nurses left, he went back to D. "You alright mate?" he asked. D was feeling light-headed, but it was a feeling he could easily brush off.

"What's with your law enforcement officials? Are they always so colorful?" D asked.

Roger just shrugged. "Well, he's always been a bit stern as to the facts rather than opinions, but he's a really nice guy once you get to know him."

D ignored that last part and closed his eyes. Roger always said that about everyone. This man really gave people the benefit of the doubt.

D's arm was still throbbing, and he felt like puking. As usual, however, he didn't have time to just sit around. He got up and started to put on his clothes.

Roger gave a small yelp at the sight of D stripping off his hospital gown, bare naked. "Oh, Good Lord!!!" he exclaimed.

D looked up while dressing. "Alright, what is it then Rog, Christian, Atheist or Odinism?" he asked.

Roger replied, "Oh, shut up! And what are you doing?" he asked.

D explained, "Well if Murray is feeding the police bull-shit about what has been happening and blaming me and my country for it, them's fightin' words!" he exclaimed, putting on his shirt.

Roger just chuckled at that last part.

D turned to Roger. "I need to borrow your car, bud," he said.

Roger came to his senses and folded his arms. He had about enough of all the secrecy going on about his new mate and demanded in a stern but questioning tone:

"Now look here.... I'm not about to... let you leave without a doctor examining you, and furthermore, we are not going anywhere until you tell me what your plan is and how I fit into all of this!!!"

D stared at Roger for a while. The old Aussie was finally starting to fight back and stand his ground. Unfortunately, it was towards the wrong man.

D looked down and chuckled a bit to himself. "I may not have my weapons on me right now, but I can assure you that I will put you out of your misery in any way you'd like! So, what'll it be?" D said.

Roger, knowing full well not to fuck with him, threw his keys at D and followed behind him. "Bloody Yanks," he muttered to himself.

CHAPTER 14

Getting past hospital staff wasn't the problem. It was getting Roger to shut his trap and not blurt out anything that would give them away.

Once they reached the old jeep, D jumped in and started to undo his bandage from the wrist and hand but not the upper arm.

As soon as he finished, he tried to start up the ignition, only for it to fail again.

"Oh, bloody fuckin' bollocks!!! Why does this shit always happen to me?!!" he complained.

D looked over to see if, once again, there was no gas, but then saw that the car didn't even have lights on despite the key being in the ignition. They both looked around to see what the problem was, Roger taking the liberty of complaining and whine the entire time about his jeep. D saw a big puddle on the ground. He looked underneath the vehicle and saw that the fuel line had been cut.

"Roger, pop the hood," he ordered.

Roger opened the jeep's hood, and D got up and took a look inside. The battery was missing.

"Do you have any enemies?" D asked.

Roger stopped his bellyaching and just shook his head. "Why do you ask mate?"

Aside from the battery, D pointed underneath and Roger saw the puddle.

"Oh, bloody hell!" he exclaimed. "Now what do we do? We've no vehicle," Roger pointed out the obvious.

D looked around, hoping to find the perp who cut the line and took the battery, but knew it was useless as it might have been done hours ago. Without his weapons, there was no way he could go back to the mine quarry. He needed to get them back.

"How far away is the police station from here?" D asked.

Roger stopped whimpering and answered, mumbling but understandable to D. "It's only a five-minute walk from here. Why?"

D explained, "I need my weapons. There's no way we can get into the mine and warn Murray without protection. How well acquainted are you with the police force?" D asked.

Roger replied, "Well I am familiar with ol Jack and Winston who work patrol down at.... Hey. Wait a Minute! You're not thinking what I think you are thinking, are you?"

Already impatient, D explained, "You know everyone around here pretty well. I just need you to get into their evidence room and get my pistol and knife... and some ammo if you can."

Roger stood his ground again. "No, No, No, No, No, there is no 'WE' this time, mate. I've been pushed around, and I've been patient so far, but now enough is enough. If you want your weapons, you're just going to have to go there yourself and get them yourself. Cause I'm not leaving!"

He folded his arms and scowled at D. "You once told me that I needed to stand up for myself. Well, here I am doing so. I'm just upset that it had to be towards you. You're always telling me that everyone acts like an asshole, but you're no better. You want people to change, maybe you're the one who needs to do so!"

D stood there looking at him like a large dog would with a chihuahua barking at him. D heard but did not care; he had a job to do.

"Well, if that's your choice and opinion, Rog, then suit yourself. I'll take care of it myself," D said, and he started off away from the hospital parking lot, leaving Roger where he stood.

Roger just stood there watching him leave, knowing full well that he needed to help, but only said what he said simply because he was terrified of what might be in that mine if they were to go any further. He also knew that though D was an asshole, he was still the one that taught him to face his fears.

He looked down at his feet and cursed and hated himself even more, knowing full well that not only was he being uncooperative when someone needed him, but also that he had lost the only friend he had come to know only a couple days ago that helped him to have some respect for himself.

CHAPTER 15

Getting into the police headquarters was not the problem. It was managing to avoid any onlookers who might think that there was a crazy lunatic with bandages on his arm and torn clothing trying to break into the building.

After hiding near a bush near the compound wall, D moved as quickly as he could to the rear of the complex to find the back door. He ducked behind the wall again when he saw two uniformed officers having their usual smoke break. He knew he could easily take them out and get inside, but it was the principle of the matter. Why hurt public officials he didn't even know? Especially during their smoke break.

"OI! You two?" he heard a voice call out. "Break's over, come inside and fill your reports on the double!" said what D thought was a superior advisor.

"Get stuffed Riley!" replied the two men, and D heard them stomp out their cigarettes, and one of them mumbled, "Fuck he thinks he is? Bloody rookie!"

D took a peek around the corner and saw that the door opened quickly but was slow to close. He also noticed that when the two started to head in, one of them left their pack of cigarettes. He didn't move, as he knew that the door might not take that long to close and if he were to move too soon, the guards would catch him.

So, he counted the seconds it took for the door to close, 'One one thousand two, three one thousand four....' he counted until it reached approximately twelve seconds, then waited for the other cop to come out and collect his pack of cigs.

It was starting to get humid again, and D was sweating all over. His bandages started to sting due to the salinity in his sweat. It was also getting him anxious as he kept looking around to make sure no one would spot him. He could see the street and the shops nearby, but it wasn't close enough that a random person, or God forbid a cop, would catch him.

D estimated that he had been waiting for about five minutes so far, and then looked to his right and saw an old wino come up to him.

"Hallo there Govena' what's all this you hidin' about for?" he asked.

He stank, and D meant STANK!

He probably slept on a pile of shit or in the garbage. D scowled.

"OH c'mon now mate, if it's all the same to ya, you don't smell any better! Why I reckon you smell like me gramps underpants, and he's dead!" the wino wheezed his laughter.

"Thanks, now move along!" D said nicely.

"Oi there, there's no need to be grumpy! I just wanted to know if ye had any drink on ya," he exclaimed.

"No, now piss off!" D said sternly.

The wino insisted, "Oh sure ya does, what with the cowboy hat and all you'd think ye was from Texas or somethin', so you lot always have somethin' hidin' in that there trousers of yours," and he reached for D's cargo pants.

D grabbed his hand with a vice-like grip, pulled the man down and covered his mouth.

"If I wasn't hurting so much right now, and more focused on getting something accomplished as well, I would break this hand, tear out your Adam's apple and shove it up that stink hole you call a 'bum.' So, unless you'd like me to do you the favor, wink once for yes and twice for no," D muttered murderously.

The wino looked as if he were pondering an answer and blinked three times.

D flicked the man's forehead and said once again, "Once for yes, twice for no!" he hissed.

The man pondered again, then looked at his captor to ask a question, and D riskily took his hand off his mouth.

"I can't count," he said proudly.

D stared at him coldly and then laughed along with him. It was one of the first laughs D had had in a while, and it came from an idiot.

By this time, both were laughing until a voice sounded off. "Hey, you two!"

They both looked up and saw what D recognized as one of the cigarette cops.

"What are you doing down there?" the officer asked.

D and the wino just looked at each other and then back to the cop.

"Deciding who should take the first shit on the wall, then wee wee their signature," D said, and both started laughing crazily.

The cop was not amused.

"Oh, a wise ass, eh? Alright you, on your feet!" the cop said.

The wino shot back, "He's not wise, he's stinky."

"What?" said the cop, and the wino further explained.

"Ya see, you called him wise ass, but his bum ain't wise he's stinky. So, call him stinky ass," and they both laughed again.

"Alright, that's enough you!" the cop said and grabbed the wino by the collar and threw him against the wall.

"I don't like winos or beggars or homeless people. In fact, I hate them so much I just can't seem to control myself when one of them's around," the cop said as he glared at him.

"Put him down, tough guy, he's harmless," D demanded. The cop drew his pistol and aimed it at D's face.

D didn't flinch, as his sights were on the cop.

"Don't you be telling me how to do my business, Yank, or

I'll show you how we do things around here," the cop replied.

"He ain't done nothing. Now let him alone," cried the wino.

The cop aimed his pistol at the man and shot him point blank in the head. Like an artist throwing red paint onto a wall, D watched as the wino's head exploded from the force of the bullet.

The officer then turned and grabbed D by the arm, the bad arm.

Normally, D would not hurt public officials, cops or military personnel unless absolutely necessary. The pain in his arm spoke for him, and D grabbed the cop by the throat, threw him against the wall, kneed him in his solar plexus, and head-butted him as hard as he could. He felt and heard the cracks of the crooked cop's jaw and teeth. The cop dropped.

With the gun going off, D knew that everyone would be rushing out to see what happened. Without thinking, he improvised. He saw the dumpster near the back door, threw himself inside and waited.

As the doors flew open, he waited and caught a peek in the crack near the corner. He saw cops running out and assessing the situation. "Holy Mother of God!" cried a female officer.

"Call an ambulance!" yelled another officer.

D waited until there was a moment of pause and then pulled off his boots and jumped out. His feet came to the ground softly as he controlled the impact.

'So much for counting,' he thought and went inside, not having any time to mourn the poor wino's fate.

All the man wanted was a drink.

CHAPTER 16

Once inside, D sped to the only place he could think of to hide for the moment. The restroom.

He saw a hallway, and to the right, thank God, there was the bathroom sign.

Right next to it was the locker room. As he entered the restroom, he went inside a stall and sat on the toilet for a while.

He was waiting for all the commotion to die down a bit and then head to the locker room to see, hopefully, that there was a spare uniform he could put on to blend in.

He couldn't get the sight out of his head. A crooked cop who killed winos and beggars for fun. It made him think about what O'Hara would have to say about it. What if O'Hara was part of it as well?

'Not my problem right now,' he thought.

When all was quiet, he slid out of the stall and headed for the door. As he looked out through the slit in the door, he saw and heard that most of the commotion was outside where the incident took place.

Taking a deep breath, he lunged out and headed for the locker room. That's when he saw the evidence room right across from it. Like all rooms with important documents and items, it required a key.

He slid into the locker room and started to look around for any uniforms lying about. He didn't have time, though; after all, it was a police station, and it wouldn't take them long to come back and do their usual business. Inside locker 422, he found a wallet, old gym shoes, and, sure enough, a uniform. God must have had mercy on him today because he found some keys on top.

Once he was dressed, he left his cowboy hat in the locker, sneaked a glance through the door to make sure no one was looking, and headed for the evidence room once the coast was clear.

There were ten keys attached to the ring, and one of them had to be the right one, as usual.

D checked each key one at a time. The first one was a no go. He then looked behind him to see if anyone was looking and then went back to work. He did this pattern six times before he found the right one. Lucky number seven.

Once he heard the click, he walked inside and closed the door softly behind him. For a small police station, the evidence room was huge. There were ten aisles worth of materials, counterfeited merchandise, weapons and one aisle strictly for drugs and narcotics. The room was so deathly quiet that he could drop a pin and it could be heard. The fan was the only thing making noise.

He searched through the weapons aisle, and there were a lot of things in the aisle that a man like him could use. Though tempted, he knew better. Good thing the aisle was alphabetized. He scrolled through and located the "F" section.

There he found his weapons all wrapped in a plastic evidence bag labeled 'Ford, Darrell.'

He geared up and made sure to at least take some extra .45mm ammo with him.

Now that he was armed, he was ready to deal damage if necessary. The only setback was still the arm, of all the war wounds he sustained over the years and he couldn't even stand a dog bite.

D opened the door quietly again and started to see if officers and medical officials were still walking back and forth.

Instead, he came face to face with an all too familiar face.

O'Hara was just about to enter the same room. They both looked at each other for three seconds, and then D grabbed him and pulled him inside to avoid any trouble. He threw the detective to the wall and covered his mouth.

D whispered, "Don't say anything and don't you dare reach for your gun. You won't need it." O'Hara just stared at him with a face of surprise and anger. "You need to calm down right now and listen to me. I am not your enemy, and I am not going to hurt you."

The detective nodded his head and D slowly took his hand off his mouth.

"What are you doing here?!" O'Hara hissed. "How on earth did you get in here aside from the obvious? Where did you get that uniform?"

D had enough. "OK, that's enough. Now shut up! You had my gear, and I simply came back to get it."

O'Hara interrupted. "This is a federal offense, Mr. Ford; you have no right to your equipment without the proper forms and clearance. Do you realize I can arrest you right here, right now?"

D wasn't fazed. "But you won't, and I'll tell you why," he said.

O'Hara looked as if he wanted to say something and then listened.

"Whatever Murray told you was a lie. He just wanted you to keep away from what the real problem is," D said.

O'Hara inquired, "What is the problem, Mr. Ford?"

D thought about what he wanted to say, but even he had trouble trying to believe it himself.

"I don't know how to explain it, and I can't make you believe me, but if you must, which I know you will, come tonight to the mine quarry and follow the trail I set for you. I'm sure there's more to this that we both don't know about. I think Murray is behind something. The only thing I can do is go back and find out for myself," D said.

O'Hara shook his head. "No, absolutely not! The mine is off-limits now to all personnel due to your accident. No one in or out."

D thought for a moment and then spoke. "I'll tell you what. This can work two ways. The first is the easiest. You let me go, and I bring you the proof that you're seeking. If I don't find it, arrest me. The second is I knock you out, take off anyway and do the same. Either way, I am leaving this room and going back. You can try and stop me, but I promise you it won't end well."

O'Hara spoke. "Is that a threat, Mr. Ford?"

D shrugged. "Call it what you want," he said.

The detective hesitated for a moment and then stood aside; he was dedicated but not stupid. He knew he wouldn't be able to take down the Texan.

D continued, "Again, meet me tonight at the mine, follow the trail and be ready. I have a bad feeling about what may be lying deep inside."

D opened the door and felt a hand on his good arm. "If you're lying, Mr. Ford, I will personally see to it that you never go back to the United States ever again."

D stared at him and replied. "Why don't you check on your police force first? After all, there are some in this precinct who love to grease out a helpless wino just because they exist. Fix your corruption first. Then we'll talk about me," D said.

He then walked out, leaving O'Hara to his thoughts about what he just told him. He headed back to the locker room and dressed back in his attire and cowboy hat. If he didn't make a move to get out now, he would be stuck.

He waited for thirty seconds before walking out double-time style, out the door and walking the opposite way to where the incident took place.

Breathing a sigh of relief, it was time to move on to the next phase of the plan: Head back to the mine.

CHAPTER 17

He called for a taxi and directed the driver where he needed to go.

Though the driver was a bit wary of an American with a Bowie knife and .45mm, he asked no questions and drove on.

It was a ten-mile drive; during that time D rested a bit.

All the excitement finally caught up to him. He closed his eyes and steadied his breathing again. Though he was much calmer now, his mind raced with many thoughts about everything that had happened so far.

Murray being an asshole, the deaths of mine workers he had witnessed, killer children and demon dogs, Rog not being any help.... 'Roger,' D Thought.

It was customary for D to be an asshole all the time and just be business as usual, but there was something deep down in his head that meant he couldn't stop thinking about how they parted. Though D wanted to justify himself as to why he was that way with Rog, he couldn't. There was no explanation or excuse for D's behavior.

Funny, was D starting to feel sympathy for Roger being who he was, or empathy knowing that D, an unruly Texan and braggart, had a heart? When this was all over, D would make amends with Roger. He deserved that much.

The car came to a stop, and D opened his eyes only to see a .357 Magnum pointed at him.

The cab driver got out on his side and walked to where D was sitting and opened it.

"Get out!" said the driver. "Put your hands in the air and get on the ground."

Staying calm, D complied and got on his knees.

"Good, now lie down on your belly and eat dirt," the driver said and kicked D in the back to do so.

D felt his front body hit the ground. His chin clipped the sand.

"Keep your hands on your head where I's can see 'em," said the driver.

He heard the man reach for a cell phone and speak.

"Yea I got 'im... sure... ah he's not so tough, gave in immediately... right... kill him and come back... yea I know the plan, no need to get testy ya fat sack of shit." He hung up on who D assumed to be Murray.

He just had a hunch it would've been him.

It was hot as hell and the outback sand only burned D's cheek.

"You stupid git! You just couldn't stay away after you was told to piss off back to America," the driver said.

D replied, "Since I'm about to die, might I know your name pardner?"

The driver spoke, "Heh sure, the names Mong but me brothers call me 'Demon Jizz.'"

D continued to look to the side with his left cheek to the sand.

"Demon Jizz, huh? They couldn't find a better name to use but jizz?" he said.

"Shut your hole!!! I like me name, it makes me powerful, and when the time is right, the dark lord will give me my reward!" the driver said.

D could tell this guy was completely nuts.

He pondered for a second and then asked, "Oh? A devil worshiper?"

"Oh, ho ho, wouldn't you like to know? Tonight, we're calling on OUR dark lord to finally give us what we've been desiring," he continued. "We all have been watching you and that idiot old man of yours. It was only a matter of time before we got the word from our leader to finally act. Ya see, tonight's the full moon, it is, and that means a new season is about to emerge, but in order to do that we needs to have a little sacrifice. That's where the old man comes in. He owns all this land, and with him out of the way we can finally take turns splittin' this land up for ourselves."

D listened to everything that was coming to frame. His attention was interrupted by 'Demon Jizz,' though.

"Oi, that's right where is he anyways?" D couldn't let Roger take the fall, so he replied.

"Well, you don't need to worry about him. I got tired of the old fart so I killed him myself."

Mong got quiet, then yelled out. "NO!!!, HE'S DEAD!!! NOW HOW ARE WE GOING TO GET THE RITUAL TO WORK? WE NEEDED HIM DAMMIT!!!"

It was all starting to come together.

While Mong called Murray again to tell him the news, D put the pieces together.

The mining accidents, the red slime, contaminated waters and Roger's National Park getting affected? This was all an elaborate scheme for fame, money, and power. Now there were devil worshippers involved.

D looked in front of him and saw something slither. A brownish light snake, assessing the area or hunting, came within inches of D's face. It just stared at him and stuck its tongue out several times to smell the huge brute that was the Texan. Slit Eyes: Dangerous, Beady Eyes: Harmless, D thought. This was Australia, though, so the fauna around here would not quite be the same as it was back in the US. D had to assume that the snake was venomous.

It got closer until it brought its head underneath D's chin, almost as if it were snuggling his goatee.

Mong kept speaking gibberish into the phone, D could not understand him. He didn't have time though; he had to act quickly.

Without thinking, he grabbed the snake with his teeth and flung it at his would-be kidnapper/murderer.

The man started to scream bloody murder as D saw the snake clamp onto his cheek with its jaws and hang on as if life depended on it. He dropped the phone, with Murray still on the line, and his revolver to try and pull the reptile off.

With the distraction happening, D turned around and jumped for the .357 revolver and, with quick aim, fired into the satanist's belly.

Like watching a watermelon explode, D was covered in blood and stared intently at the man, who was flung back at the intensity and speed of the bullet, sprawled over about ten feet away.

No need to assess if he was still alive or not. He'd seen damage like this before and knew that his place in Hell was now being occupied.

D got to his feet and wiped his face with napkins that the now-deceased Mong left in the cab. He then proceeded to grab his belongings and stow away his newly acquired weapon.

"Oi, you pissant, you still there?" yelled a voice on the dropped cell phone.

D picked up the phone and listened. "You kill him or not? What was that noise? You'd better have killed him, or you'll be flayed alive!" Murray spat into the phone.

D paused for a second and then spoke two words that he knew Murray, of all people, would understand. "That's... three..." D said murderously.

He could have sworn he heard choking on the other end of the line before he heard, "Oh Shit!" and the phone cut off.

He was about to drop the phone, then thought of an idea.

He threw the phone onto the passenger side of the cab and turned the ignition. He drove for the road and passed by the remains of 'Demon Jizz', whose face looked as if he had no idea what had just happened.

CHAPTER 18

It wasn't difficult getting back to the mine by himself.

He had memorized the roads and street signs that aligned towards the destination.

In order for him to remain inconspicuous, he hid Mong's cab a few yards away from the gate entrance and walked the rest of the way.

It was pitch dark now. In Australia, when night time comes it definitely gets dark. The only positive outlook was that the stars were shining brightly.

The entire compound of the Smithston Mine was completely dead. Not a soul in sight as he looked through the fence. Just like O'Hara told him.

He still searched around to make sure there were no guards or employees on site.

Once clear, he took off his tactical boots and tied the shoelaces together. He then placed them around the front of his neck, the boots hanging from his back.

With careful precision and silence, he climbed over the fence, starting with his right hand and left foot first, then alternating with the others. An alligator crawl he learned during the military that helped increase speed with minimal noise.

As he was climbing down from the other side of the fence, D looked to his right side towards the foreman's office.

Murray's office.

There were other cars parked there, about five. No lights on in the building though.

Where are they?

He placed his boots back on and saw an old tree that had been cut down due to construction, and approached it looking for an old thick branch he could use. D found two the length of his entire arm.

He then took his Bowie knife out and carved the end of one stick to form a sharp wooden blade, which took him thirty minutes to do. He then tested the point on his thumb with a soft touch, blood trickling out of the open skin.

Perfect.

He then sheathed his knife and approached one of the cars.

Fortunately, one of the cars was a truck and carried an extra gas can for emergencies. He also found an empty canteen with a strap attached.

He then took the gas can and poured a little on the wooden blade, making sure that the blade was soaked with the gasoline. He then poured more into the canteen.

Since he had no flashlight this time, he had to make a torch to see through the mine once he went in. The plus side would be that the torch would also serve as a sharp weapon temporarily should he come across any trouble.

He then pulled out a lighter that he happened to sneak from the evidence room back at the police station and lit the torch.

He then took a huge breath and approached the mine.

Tonight would determine whether he had what it takes to fight off monsters and demons, or if his luck had finally run out.

CHAPTER 19

An eerie vibe set the mood of the mine already, but at night it gave it a more terrifying feel.

For D it was just another walk in the park. The only difference was that instead of human enemies, these were not of this world or probably dimension.

That didn't matter now. He was a soldier after all, expendable. If he died today, who would mourn? Roger? Overstreet? Nah, he knew that if he died, he would easily be replaced by another soldier of fortune. That's how it works, no time to cry.

He saw one of the mine carts in the distance from the light of the torch. Murray's. It sat right where the red slime started to form, but no further. Murray was an idiot, but knew better than to take his cart deeper. After all, whatever could come out of the slime could definitely ruin his transportation method.

It's a good thing that D made marks in the dirt with the other stick that displayed his path; otherwise how would O'Hara know where to go?

That's if he showed up.

D moved forward, the light directing his path with his pistol at the ready. His skin tightened as he felt the humid air all around him. No sound whatsoever, just his footsteps. 'A normal person would be shitting their pants right now,' D thought, but his gaze and eyes were set on finding the gold mine, which was the hideout for these demon worshippers.

It was too quiet.

D had been walking through the mine now for about ten

minutes. All he heard was silence.

He noticed that the slime was starting to pulsate, going from a dark red to a light pink hue on and off. He wondered if he needed the torch after all, but didn't trust the slime at all.

He heard a moan from far away, like a man crying for nourishment. It faded. Another cry came out, and this time it sounded like a child crying for mercy. Almost like it was being beaten to death. It too, faded. The low moan came back, followed by the child's cry again. It repeated on and off until more voices started to call out. They were surrounding D, one after the other.

He kept moving forward though, despite what he was hearing, his stern face still set on his mission.

They were getting louder, almost to the point of deafening.

The slime too was starting to move its color back and forth rapidly.

Though determined, D stopped in his tracks and closed his eyes.

Concentrating on setting his mind to block out the horrendous voices from Hell.

He didn't even see figures start to emerge from the slime one by one, reaching for D as he stood still and allowed his arms to be at his side.

Mangled, gnarled hands and bodies creeping towards this lonely Texan.

D started to say the Lord's prayer in his head over and over again.

The cadavers' hands started to grab his legs and arms, touching his body from top to bottom.

He felt everything, from slime to ragged flesh, and the cries and moans continued.

Louder they got. So loud the mine could collapse on him any minute from the volume of sounds.

He maintained focus on his prayer.

Suddenly, like the snap of fingers, it stopped.

He didn't feel the hands anymore either.

He opened his eyes... nothing.

The slime was still pulsating on and off, but at its regular intervals.

D raised his pistol and torch and started moving forward again. Making sure to mark every line in the ground for O'Hara.

Five minutes later, he was now in an area of the mine he had not been to before, a small cavern with mine carts that had not been touched for months, from what D thought. Inside each cart were different sorts of minerals and uranium ore that had not been broken down yet. There were ladders and man-made bridges and walkways that had long been abandoned.

The slime surrounded the entire cavern, but surprisingly wasn't dripping.

There were three tunnels: the one D came from, the second on the second floor to his right, and the third on the top floor straight ahead. He made his way to the makeshift ladder, holstered his pistol and climbed up, torch still in hand.

Taking care once again to not touch the walls, he carefully stepped to the first walkway on the second floor.

He came to the tunnel and was surprised to see that there was no slime through that tunnel. He also saw that it was a dead end. Only one other place to go, and that was up.

Taking care to climb the other ladder once more and repeat the same obstacles, he made his way to the last tunnel on top.

He then shined his light to walk in and was met with a six-foot-tall creature that closely resembled a deformed, hairless goat standing on its hind legs. It had sunken dark eyes, long fangs hanging from its top jaws, and was brandishing a huge ax.

That was all D needed to see as he ducked from the ax, swinging to take his head off and rolled to his left flank, letting go of the torch.

He drew his pistol and aimed, but there was nothing there.

He then heard a low guttural bleat, an ungodly sound that D had never heard before. It sounded as if it were coming from the other side of the cavern.

Could it move that fast?

D reached for the torch and shined all over the place but saw nothing.

The cavern was now pitch black.

The bleating continued.

'SWICK,' D felt a tear in his back.

"UGHGGGRR!" D growled in pain.

He turned and fired a round but saw that it was in vain as nothing was there.

Again, the terrible bleating sound was all around the cavern. His back was starting to stick with freshly coated blood and hurt like hell.

D regained focus and shined the light again all over the place.

He heard a sloshing sound from his left, but once he turned, he was met with a kick to the cheek.

"AAHHHH!!!" D cried in pain and anger. This was not going to go well if he continued to just stay in one place, but where could he go?

Mind racing, he thought of one idea. It was one in a million, but he had to try.

He holstered his pistol. He then listened, trying to concentrate on his breathing. Silence again. Then he heard in the distance that the bleating began again.

D started to assess the situation as quickly as he could. If he didn't focus, he was a dead man. He listened for any other noises in the area that could compromise his goal of killing this creature. He had been doing this all of his military years. Check surroundings for any more targets but use it to get an idea of what made the enemy or enemies stand out.

He sought out anything he could hear. The sloshing noises,

the swish of the wind if the creature came by, the hooves clomping around or.... That's IT! The sloshing sounds! The fucker was using the slime to get back and forth at D.

He waited in a kneeling position, gripping the torch tightly. Silence all around him. He stared forward, spat out blood, and listened carefully. A slush happened behind him again.

Without knowing where he might strike, he dropped to his back and raised his torch quickly into the air, where it was met with a 'CHUNK!'

The demon cried out in pain as D, with a look of vengeance and anger, plunged the torch/spear deeper into its belly. Dark ooze dripped from the wound.

With one hand, D brought out his pistol and fired four shots into the chin of the creature. He brought his enemy to the ground, the bleating now a disturbing cry.

He then reached for the ax the monster dropped and picked it up. 'Good God, it's heavy,' D thought, and with both hands raised the ax and brought it down to the demon's neck.

The head rolled only an inch while the gurgling sound of its cries was starting to fade. "Asshole!" D said with the utmost disgust.

"Hello, sweets!" D heard a female voice.

He then felt pressure in his back where he had his injury.

"GRRRRR," he growled again in pain, but as he spun around to deck the broad in the face, another fist closed in on his cheek. The same cheek where he was kicked.

He fell to the ground; he was exhausted. He felt a foot turn him over on his back, and then was planted on top of his chest.

All D could see were two cloaked figures, a male and female. His eyes were blurry, though.

He then saw the woman's foot rise to his face, and she stamped hard. D only saw darkness.

CHAPTER 20

His arms were sore, and he opened his eyes.

His vision was still blurry, but he knew where he was, or at least his body told him where he was.

He felt the feeling before.

He was hanging from a ten-ton wire connected to a crane. He was also hovering over a pit. A very dark, deep pit.

D wondered how the workers or cultists got a ten ton crane down in the cavern in the first place.

Despite his blurriness, he scanned his surroundings carefully. His head still throbbed from that bitch who kicked him in the face.

Good thing the wire twirled around. He moved his body slightly and saw that he was in an even bigger cavern. How big was this mining facility, D wondered.

He twirled slowly and faced the crane itself. There was the answer. This cavern must have been closest to the surface up top. There was a huge opening from the top that allowed the gravel to slant down which could have allowed the workers to bring the crane down. Of course, that opening could have been done with dynamite.

He thought to himself, perhaps O'Hara could sneak in from there, but as he looked closely as best as he could, he saw a glowing red substance. Slime. Unless O'Hara had a death wish, D knew he wouldn't be stupid enough to try and penetrate it. Then again he didn't know the detective all that well either.

He felt a bead of sweat slide down his forehead. He realized his hat was gone along with his weapons. They took them, even his hat.

'You bastards,' D said in his head. Never touch a Texan's hat without their blessing. That was the ultimate sin in D's book.

As his eyesight slowly returned, he saw that he was surrounded all along the pit by the same cloaked figures. He counted about twenty of them, male and female.

The crane turned on and the wire started to move D towards what he assumed was the leader of the group.

A female. From the looks of her she seemed about her late thirties, maybe forties. She definitely worked out as he could see her body figure. The cloak embraced her. If she wasn't evil, D might have been interested. Then again, she was most likely the same woman who stomped his face.

Looks or no looks, D would remind himself to kill her later, when this was all over.

Funny, he seemed to think he was getting out of this alive.

The wire got him about a foot away from her, and then she lifted off her hood.

No wonder D might have been interested; it was the same woman from Murray's office.

The "Teacher!" The "Doctor!" The BITCH! No wonder she rubbed him the wrong way in Murray's office. He remembered the scene as she walked past him and brushed his arm. The tension in his right arm, the bad arm. He was marked! She caused all of this to happen to D. The interference in his dreams, the zombies taking the forms of former enemies he killed long ago.

She looked at D seductively, a smirk forming on her lips. She then placed a hand on his chest and started to caress him. She then spoke, "Sorry love, didn't mean to kick you so hard. But at least I've still got you whole... for now."

The other cloaked figures were just standing around the

pit, paying no attention to D and the woman.

D just stared at her with a poker face that could have been a resemblance of a scowl and a form of concentration.

"Nothing to say?" she asked, stroking his face and chin.

She then stopped and pulled out a knife. "Good, then this will be over quickly for you, my dear. Too bad, I would've given you one for free," she said, then she grabbed him by the collar and licked his lips.

D growled like a fighter pit bull wanting to maul.

She took a few steps back and addressed her followers.

"This court is now in session!" she spoke loudly.

In a militaristic manner, every cloaked figure turned and stared at D, who was being moved away back to the center of the pit.

"Behold, the shadow of the moon protects us, its cooling, soothing darkness enveloping us. For like us all, we too have a shadow that serves as our counterpart. A hole within us all, waiting, longing to be filled with the power of our dark lord," she chanted. The followers started to chant with her as well.

D couldn't understand them, but it was all in unison and monotonous.

The woman continued, "Oh, dark guardian from the world we seek. With this sacrifice we so willingly give to you, let us feel the power of your fury. Let us drink off the blood of this lamb and become forever your humble servants!"

Though D was now coming to his senses fully, he still had no strength or energy to think clearly. Even if he were to get loose, he was ten feet away from solid ground. He felt himself stop twirling and was facing away from the crane. He then saw the woman walk forward over the pit, as if there was an invisible bridge. No, not walking, more like floating.

'Is that even possible?' D thought.

The followers were chanting louder.

Once she was face to face with D, she leaned forward and spoke into his ear. "This could end really quickly for you. All you have to do is pledge yourself to me. Be my slave, and I will let you live. With me, my family, and your new god."

She pulled herself to be nose-to-nose with him, smiling and waiting for an answer. The chanting continued. D stared into her eyes, and hers into his. She then took the knife and made a small incision near his heart. D continued to stare, despite the pain.

She moved back to his ear.

"Yes, it was me by the way. I am the one who made you see all those horrific visions. The forms inside the mine. You are a very dark person, Mr. Ford."

She plunged the knife tip a bit deeper. D sneered.

She continued, "I know all about you now, all those terrible things that you've done in life. I can take all that away. Just say the word and it will stop."

She brought her body closer to his. She started to rub her cheek with his and lightly touch her lips. "You see, I have a power, a force that can make people suffer. That's what I did to you in the office. I did it because I like you. I want you. Be mine."

She stared at him again, and he continued to stare into oblivion.

She then raised her hands up, and all was silent.

"What is your answer?" she asked and again licked his lips.

With a sudden jerk, he opened his mouth and bit down on her tongue.

He jerked to his right and tore it out. He then spat it out.

"Go to Hell!" he said and raised his legs up and kicked her square in the chest.

Perhaps she must have been distracted because her invisible bridge was now an invisible nothing.

She screamed in pain and horror as she fell down into the pit. Knife included.

Her followers were now screaming and cursing at D as their leader was now dead at the bottom of the pit.

There was a particular follower who seemed to be second in command. He yelled out to the operator on the crane to lower the chain. The crane operator then reached for the control console and was about to press the release button when a familiar cry to D sounded off.

"OI MATE! DON'T YOU WORRY! HELP IS ON THE WAAAAAAAAYYYYY!!!"

CHAPTER 21

Roger came rushing in, screaming bloody murder as he fired a familiar bracelet into the crowd.

Behind him was none other than O'Hara and two detectives following suit.

"RIGHT! PUT YOUR HANDS IN THE AIR! NOBODY MOVE A FUCKIN' MUSCLE!"

The followers dispersed rapidly.

It was every man for himself now.

Roger rushed at the crane operator and tackled him to the ground. He then grabbed a rock and hit him over the head, knocking him out.

The others apparently had weapons of their own as they started firing at O'Hara and his two partners.

"I'M COMING FOR YA D!" Roger screamed as he made the wire come to the left side of the crane.

He placed D down, and from there he collapsed.

"Oh no! Not again!" Roger stated as he noticed the wound near D's heart. He rushed to pick up his best friend. "Come on now, come on. You're not going to die. I won't let you!" he exclaimed as he gave D some water from a canteen he carried. D didn't move. "Mate, don't do this to me. I'm sorry for walkin' out on ya. I promise from now on, I'm gonna stick by your side no matter what!" he said with tears in his eyes.

"Roger..." he heard D say.

Roger listened.

"Can I just... close my eyes for a bit... I'm fucking tired," D said weakly but with a slight smirk.

Roger laughed. "Sleep when you're dead, mate. Isn't that what they say in the Marines?" he asked.

"Close enough," D said.

He got up and prepared for battle.

"Oi mate, you need these," Roger said and handed him the bracelet, a black hatchet and his cowboy hat. "The fuckers left it on the crane," Roger said.

D clapped him on his shoulder and said, "Thanks bro!" Then he hurried off to help O'Hara.

Before he could, though, there was rumbling happening from within the pit, and everyone stopped in their tracks. From the inside of the pit came a red flashing aura. D knew better and told Roger to get behind one of the boulders near the crane.

Suddenly, red slime started to spray from the pit all around, and a hideous creature emerged from within.

Like King Kong rising from his jungle abode, this monster was taller than the first. Its height was about twelve feet tall and resembled a reptilian pig-like creature. D named it a Snig. Crappy name, but it was all he could think of at the time. It had no weapons, not that it needed any. The fangs, claws and muscles made up for it.

D now knew what made the footprints during his first investigation.

Did the slime produce this abomination, or was this their dark lord?

Everyone just stared at the monstrosity as it lumbered out of the pit covered in red slime. It moved its head around to observe all the humans surrounding it, snorting and hissing.

"HOLY SHIT! RUN!" cried one of the cultists.

The monster then turned its head quickly towards the culprit and roared an inhuman sound.

O'Hara and his comrades fell back behind a boulder while the followers were running around to escape.

It was no use, the exit out of the cavern was sealed by slime.

D saw one of the cultists melt inside the doorway, screaming in pain and terror.

The monster was taking turns grabbing each follower and devouring them or killing them for pleasure. One follower tripped and fell to the ground. The creature raised a foot and stomped down on his waist. He cried in pain as blood spurted from his mouth. The "Snig" reached down, tore his upper torso off and shoved it in its mouth.

D was leading Roger from boulder to boulder, staying out of sight. Some cultists had the nerve to try their luck in killing D and Roger, but the Texan was quicker.

One ambushed them from above. D pushed Roger out of the way and, with quick precision, grabbed the cultist by the arms and threw him down. He then took the hatchet and hammered it on his head. Roger gasped in horror but knew it was either them or him.

Another follower ran at D with a knife. D grabbed the dead body from the handle of the hatchet and held it in front of him. The female follower stabbed the body before she could get D. He then reached around his human shield, grabbed her by the hair and pulled her towards him. He then chopped her throat with his hand and smashed her face on the boulder. Either she was dead or not going to be happy in the morning.

"Oh, come on now, the woman had to snuff it too?" Roger complained. D grabbed him and rushed forward.

More started to come at both of them. D finally had a chance to try Roger's invention.

He fired a volley of bullets in their direction and mowed them down one by one. "Fuckin A," D stated. He turned to Roger and gave him a thumbs up.

Almost all of the followers were dead, either by the red slime, D or the Snig killing them.

D heard the second-in-command follower bellow out from the top of his lungs. "KENAI UTOM!" The Snig stopped and stared at its caller. "BIUSTA CRIANDA!" he yelled and pointed at D. The Snig starred in the Texan's direction and roared. D mumbled, "Shit!" and he and Roger ran for their lives.

D yelled for Roger to take cover and hide. Roger didn't question and ran for it. The creature was still running for D. He was hauling ass as quickly as he could, but the monster was gaining momentum.

A quick idea rushed in, but it would only work if the scenario happened. Sure enough, the Snig pounced to try and catch D.

The Texan then stopped and jumped in the opposite direction, towards the monster. As he hit the floor, he could have sworn he heard the behemoth grunt, "HUH?" in confusion. The Snig landed on a huge boulder and fell to the side.

D got up and looked quickly around him and found a weapon of use. He found a hydraulic water jet gun the size of a cannon connected to a rig next to the crane and ran towards it. The keys were still in the ignition, and he turned it on, followed by an on switch.

The rig started to warm up. The monster was coming to its senses and looked around to find its target.

D growled, "Hurry up you useless piece of crap!"

The Snig found him and charged forward. The pit was in front of it, so D still had seconds to wait. To his horror, though, the creature jumped forward and over the pit with arms and jaws wide open. It was now or never.

D held on to the water cannon and pressed the trigger, praying to God that it would work.

Everything seemed to happen in slow motion. The Snig jumped over the pit as the cannon kicked into life and fired a thick stream of water into the belly of the beast. D felt kicked back as well as the pressure of the water and machine recoiled. The water was moving at a very high speed, and it pushed the Snig back to where it jumped from.

As it fell back, D released the trigger and waited to see if it was dead. It didn't move for a bit, but eventually it rose slowly. That's when D caught what he was looking for. The machine made a huge hole in the beast's stomach, intestines and organs dripping out. The Snig looked at the damage, then at D and roared again.

D didn't wait.

He fired again at the beast's arm and tore it off with the water jet. The creature screamed in pain as the arm fell off to its side.

D prepared to aim for the head, but then felt a stabbing pain in his back wound again.

The cultist who now controlled the beast was right behind him, stopping him from doing any more damage.

D turned and smacked him in the face with his right backhand.

As the follower fell to the ground, the cloak came off and revealed a furious and bloody-nosed Murray.

"It's over, you slimy piece of shit!" D called out to him.

"YOU FUCKIN' BASTARD! YOU'VE RUINED EVERYTHING!!!" he roared and charged at D, tackling him down.

The Snig was very angry that there was a hole in its stomach and now missing an arm. It roared again and prepared to charge, until a voice cried out.

"OI YOU!"

The monster looked behind him and saw a terrified Roger raising his fists at the Snig.

"YEA YA STUPID BLOODY TIT! COME AND GET ME!" Roger cried and ran off.

The Snig grunted and pursued.

O'Hara, who had been watching everything but couldn't believe it himself, yelled at Roger.

"ARE YOU FUCKING STUPID MAN?!! GET OUT OF IT'S WAY!!!" he screamed.

Roger, who was running and dodging bodies and rocks, hollered back, "NO! FORD NEEDS HELP, SHOOT IT!!! SHOOT IT!!!"

O'Hara called on his detective partners, who raised their firearms and started firing at the Snig's head.

The Snig, being annoyed at the bullets, turned and spat a vomit-like substance at them.

They ducked and watched a boulder that the vomit landed on melt.

Roger and O'Hara took turns distracting the creature while D settled his feud with Murray.

CHAPTER 22

Murray was a big man who could hold his own, but against a military vet and special forces agent, he was no match. Every punch swung only hit air as D continued to move out of the way.

Murray charged again but was met with D's right fist. He fell back and spat out more blood.

D picked him up by the collar and brought him face to face with him. Murray didn't look so tough anymore; he almost looked as if he were in a trance. D just stared at him with hate and contempt.

Murray spoke finally, "Fuck... you... and... go to... Hell!"

D aimed the bracelet at Murray's chin and replied, "You First!" As he pressed the trigger, he saw Murray's head blow apart like a pumpkin.

He stood up and took a huge breath of relief until he heard Roger cry out to him.

"D! HELP!!! I CAN'T HOLD IT OFF ANY LONGER!!!"

D turned around and grabbed the water jet. The Snig caught up to Roger, who was lying on the ground in horror, and was about to smash him with its remaining arm. D fired the jet and caught the creature in the back of the neck.

The Snig became stunned as blood started to drip out of its mouth. Roger saw the flesh peeling from its neck as its head fell off and was about to land on him. He rolled out of the way as the head crashed down. The body dropped to its knees and fell to the side.

Roger got up, looked at the body and then the head and then spat on it.

"That'll teach ya!" he said. He then turned and waved at D, who waved back with a small smirk of exhaustion.

O'Hara came out from where he and his partners were stationed, and all looked as the monster started to melt into the slime. Then the rest of the slime started to dissipate and disappear. The slime that was in the pit started to sink away until there was nothing left but a normal pit.

O'Hara walked up to Roger and shook his hand. "You are one crazy son of a bitch," he stated.

Roger shrugged and replied, "Well, what can I say? I learned from the Texan," he said as he pointed in D's direction.

There was no one there, though.

Roger and O'Hara looked at each other, and all of them rushed towards the water cannon.

There, lying right next to the remains of Murray, was D. His body was not moving. Both feared the worst.

Waves of crystal-clear blue ocean calmly hit the sand. A cool breeze swept through the air. He was lying down on the sand, lifeless and pale. Despite this, he could still listen. He could hear voices, gentle tones that mirrored an image of angels singing in chorus. His soul was ready. He was ready to move on. A soothing voice spoke to him. 'It's not your time. They need you. Find them....'

He awoke on a stretcher inside the ambulance. His vision was once again blurry, as the figures all around him were glossy.

He heard one voice, though.

"Hang in there mate, we'll get you the help you need."

Such a good man Roger was. He came back for D, though deep down inside, D didn't deserve it. He had been a cold man since he got to Australia, or should he say all of his life? This was the first person who ever showed D human compassion, and all he could do was push it away.

He gave a small thumbs up to Roger. He smiled back and gave him one as well.

He then closed his eyes and sank into a nice and much-needed deep sleep.

CHAPTER 23

Had all that really happened? Did he witness something super-natural and unbelievable?

He had so many questions.

He lay in his hospital bed. His usual demeanor would be to get up and get out as quickly as possible. This time though, he just rested.

A door opened and D saw Roger and O'Hara walk in.

Roger had several goodie bags that the nurses gave him to give to D, since this time D was being a good patient.

"Morning mate. What's the good word?" Roger asked.

D sat up with the assistance of O'Hara.

"Oh, you know, just having a good lie down... pondering my escape move... how am I going to go back to the mine? The usual," he said.

Roger just stared at him in disbelief.

D just shrugged. "Sorry dude, I gotta go back and see if everything is clear," D insisted.

O'Hara cleared his voice and spoke up, "Not to worry, Mr. Ford, I'll have you know that my men and I searched all over the place and even inside the mine," he said. "Not a soul in sight, and the red slime has disappeared. Once we give the OK, all the workers can return to work with a new supervisor. All's well that ends well!" he stated.

D looked at O'Hara. "You believe me now?" he asked.

O'Hara shrugged.

"Well, in a world like the one we live in, who's to say what you might find out there in the darkness of the human soul?

I guess all my time of being a police officer and experiencing things such as robberies, homicides, and even terrorist situations, nothing, and I mean nothing, could have ever prepared me for what I saw last night. You know, my mother used to tell me that God always worked in mysterious ways and that when the time was right, He would show me what was right and wrong. I was wrong about you, Mr. Ford; I see now that words and politics can easily manipulate and influence any individual into believing something that isn't there. Murray had a lot of connections to many colorful people. We are looking into them right now. But the ones that we witnessed, these loony cultists, that was something new for me that I feel will never escape my head," he said.

D nodded his head in agreement. Roger just looked down and fidgeted a little bit.

"You OK, Rog?" D asked.

Roger looked up and said, "That was the first time I ever stood up for myself in front of a beast like that. Never in all my life could I have done somethin' of that sort. Am I changing?" he asked D.

D replied, "Well... everyone changes for good or bad. The question you should ask yourself is, what do you choose to do with this change?"

Roger smiled and thought for a minute. "Yea you're right.... Oh, fuck, I've got to get to work. It's been three days since I've been there. See you soon, D," he said and rushed out like a bat out of hell.

Both men shook their heads in humor, and D took a breath before breaking the ice.

"You know a lot of people have died these past couple of days. I killed some of them," he said. He looked at O'Hara and asked, "Will you come for me when my time is done here?"

O'Hara looked uncomfortable with that question and thought for a moment. He sat down on a comforter chair and spoke.

"The way I see it... was all self-defense really. Sure, Murray was a big man who knew people, but once word goes around about how he managed the place...." he paused to think and then spoke, "a mining accident, right? A mining accident that caused several others and eventually himself to meet the same fate," he said.

He then went further. "As for the fellow cab driver whom we found in the desert not too far away from the compound, I believe he was named... Mong? Well, there's your self-defense. You have suffered much, Mr. Ford, and now that I have seen exactly what you were investigating in the first place. I find no cause to bring you in on any charges or questioning," he said as he smiled.

D laid back and stared at the ceiling, satisfied with the verdict and that O'Hara had his back in cleaning up this mess and everything else.

"Furthermore, Mr. Ford. Should you continue any further in our beautiful country on your investigation for your American Government, do tell me of your whereabouts before doing so," he finished.

"You bet, Sarge!" D agreed.

As O'Hara got up to leave, he paused in the doorway.

"Sarge..." he said aloud. "Not too shabby, but don't get used to it," he replied.

As he turned to walk out of the room, he stopped suddenly and reached into his coat.

"Oh yes, I forgot about this." He walked over and handed D his bowie knife that the cultists had taken from him.

D's eyes widened. He thought that when he was given the black hatchet that his knife was gone.

"Might want to keep that with you at all times mate. This is Australia, and our terrain can be very treacherous...but then again you already knew that didn't you?" O'Hara said and he walked out of the room.

As D lay there holding his blade and inspecting it for any chips or knicks, he thought about everything that had transpired so far.

He had seen many things on his missions across the world. Most of which had been in other countries with situations such as out-of-control dictators that needed to be quelled discreetly, terrorists in South America that held babies and children at their mercy for trade, and he remembered before this current assignment rescuing a Korean scientist from the darkest bowels of a North Korean prison.

This, however, was a first in the supernatural realm.

Then it finally clicked in his head.

This was real!

There is life after death, and there are deranged societies bent on making pacts with the devil himself.

He then remembered his conversation with Roger when they had first met. "Do you believe in ghosts?" D recalled in his mind. The old coot was right all along. Except in this case: Monsters and demons. It still didn't sit well with D but he now accepted it.

The dreams he had been having as well made him question his sanity. Or had they only happened because of the events that had happened around the mine?

He thought about the red slime and the things that came out of it.

The little girl, the demon dog, the zombie, the cult, and the Snig?

His out-of-body experience also played a factor, and the voice telling him to 'find them.'

But who's them?

As a mercenary, his job was strictly on following orders and nothing more. Do the job and come home. Yet something was telling D that there's more to this situation and more than meets the eye. It was a pull on him. Thoughts of whether or not he should return now to the United States or remain where he was?

However, he asked himself two questions that could easily influence that decision.... 'Is this over? Or is it just the beginning?'

...TO BE CONTINUED

Acknowledgments

To Diana Dominguez and Corey Trahan. Two people in my life who helped me with this project financially. Without your help and support, this series would never have come to fruition. Thank you so much!

To Jake and Anjanette Koehler. I don't have many friends, but y'all definitely gave me that push that I needed in my life to make my dreams come true. From listening a bit to the first couple of drafts to just giving me the advice I needed for direction in life, you are truly the best friends I ever had. Love Y'all!

To my family. Mom and Dad, you have supported me and lifted me in so many ways that I cannot begin to thank you for it. Thank you for never giving up on me. My brothers and sister: Bobby, Marco, Mario and Victoria. Parts of this book are based on ideas and adventures we all had as kids. Imagination is a beautiful thing. Thank you all for your input all these years.

To my other family members not bound by blood. Kimberley Jean and Levi Jackson, Tricia and Gzmo, Zac and Amanda Gamm, Danielle and Trent Calhoun, Pete Cantu, Ace and Erica Xavier, John Melody and Natalie Najvar, Kevin Sauceda, Michelle Moffit and Kevin Smith and Jennifer Nilsson. Thank you for your interest in wondering what will come next for D and for starting the first unofficial Texan fan club. Y'all are truly amazing and loved!

To Jason Valdez and Orlando Campa. Thank you for your artwork and time in reading the story and filling the reader in on what's to come ahead. I am proud and honored to call you both my brothers.

Finally, to everyone else who has come into my life and I into theirs: Lost Pines Cowboy Church, Bat City Scaregrounds, Ratchetdolls and anyone else I forgot. You are the best and amazing! My influences and ideas have come about because of your friendship, guidance and overall fun-filled adventures!

Special Thanks to two men whom I identify with the most for helping me create The Texan himself. Dimebag Darrell of Pantera and famous actor Harrison Ford.

Love y'all, and see you on the next adventure for Darrell Ford.

About Atmosphere Press

Founded in 2015, Atmosphere Press was built on the principles of Honesty, Transparency, Professionalism, Kindness, and Making Your Book Awesome. As an ethical and author-friendly hybrid press, we stay true to that founding mission today.

If you're a reader, enter our giveaway for a free book here:

SCAN TO ENTER
BOOK GIVEAWAY

If you're a writer, submit your manuscript for consideration here:

SCAN TO SUBMIT
MANUSCRIPT

And always feel free to visit Atmosphere Press and our authors online at atmospherepress.com. See you there soon!

About the Author

Daniel Olivarez was born in McAllen, Texas, where he attended James "Nikki" Rowe High School and graduated from the University of Texas Pan American with a Bachelor of Arts in Music. As a musician, he is well versed in playing and teaching all instruments, but his favorites are saxophone and guitar for his personal company D's Music Studio. An avid rocker and metal head at heart, he enjoys going to live concerts and gracing the stage with other bands and musician friends.

Olivarez started his passion for writing when he would imagine different scenarios and characters related to them and write down what he would think are screenplays or scripts. It wasn't until 2014 that he decided to put his writing skills to the test and introduce one of his most beloved characters to his family and friends: Darrell Ford, AKA "D". As a first-time author, his influences range from different writers—Stephen King, Michael Crichton—to comic book creators such as Bob Kane with Bill Ward of Batman, to filmmakers Steven Spielberg and Sam Raimi.

When not working, Olivarez loves to spend time with his fur babies Coco and Lita or to be out traveling. His destinations include Arizona, Florida, Hawaii, Louisiana, Nevada, and Oregon. He loves motorcycles and is usually riding his Harley Davidson when visiting his hometown of McAllen.